School's Out!

RACHEL YODER—
Always Trouble Somewhere

Book 1

WANDA &
BRUNSTETTER

BARBOUR
PUBLISHING

All Pennsylvania Dutch words are taken from the *Revised Pennsylvania German Dictionary* found in Lancaster County, Pennsylvania.

Cover artist: Richard Hoit

For more information about Wanda E. Brunstetter, please access the author's Web site at the following Internet address: www.wandabrunstetter.com

This book is a work of fiction. Names, characters, places, and incidents are either products of the author's imagination or used fictitiously. Any similarity to actual people, organizations, and/or events is purely coincidental.

Published by Barbour Publishing, Inc., P.O. Box 719, Uhrichsville, Ohio 44683, www.barbourbooks.com

Our mission is to publish and distribute inspirational products offering exceptional value and biblical encouragement to the masses.

Member of the
Evangelical Christian
Publishers Association

Printed in the United States of America.

Dedication

To my son, Richard Jr., who had his share of fun
with lightning bugs when he was a boy.

And to my grandchildren: Richelle, Philip, and Ric,
who, like Rachel Yoder, enjoy doing many fun
things on their mini-farm.

Other books by Wanda E. Brunstetter

Children's Fiction

Rachel Yoder—Always Trouble Somewhere Series
The Wisdom of Solomon

Adult Fiction

Sisters of Holmes County Series
Brides of Webster County Series
Daughters of Lancaster County Series
Brides of Lancaster County Series
White Christmas Pie

Nonfiction

Wanda E. Brunstetter's Amish Friends Cookbook
The Simple Life

Glossary

ach—oh
aldi—girlfriend
baremlich—terrible
bensel—silly child
bletsching—spanking
blicking—shelling
boppli—baby
bruder—brother
bussli—kitten
busslin—kittens
butzemann—scarecrow
daadihaus—grandfather's house
daed—dad
danki—thank you
dumm—dumb
dunner—thunder
fleh—fleas
galgedieb—scoundrel
gretzich—crabby
gut—good
jah—yes
kapp—cap
kinner—children
kischblich—silly
kotze—vomit
lecherlich—ridiculous
mamm—mom

maus—mouse
naerfich—nervous
rutschich—squirming
schnell—quickly
schweschder—sister
verhuddelt—confused
wedderleech—lightning
wunderbaar—wonderful

"Das Lob Lied"
Der Herr sie gedankt.
Em Tom sei hutschle bin ich leedich.
Gebscht uff?
Guder mariye.
Immer druwwle eiyets.
Kens devun hot's duh kenne.

"The Hymn of Praise"
Thank the Lord.
I'm tired of Tom's neighing.
Do you give up?
Good morning.
Always trouble somewhere.
Neither one could do it.

Contents

Introduction

The Amish are a group of people who, due to their religious beliefs, live a plain life without the use of many modern tools. Early Amish people lived in Europe, but many came to America in the 1700s so they could worship freely. More than 150,000 Amish now live in the United States and Canada.

The Old Order Amish wear plain clothes, much like the American pioneers used to wear. Because they believe electricity is too modern, they use kerosene, propane gas, coal, diesel fuel, and wood for heating their homes, cooking, and running their machinery and appliances. Telephones are not allowed inside their houses, but some Amish have phones in their shops, barns, or sheds outside the home. Most Amish use a horse and buggy for transportation, but they ride in cars with hired drivers to take longer trips and go places where they can't drive their buggies.

At one time, most Amish men farmed for a living, but now many work as blacksmiths, harness makers, carpenters, painters, and in other trades. Some Amish women earn money by selling eggs, fruits and vegetables, or handmade items such as dolls and quilts. Others work in gift shops, bakeries, or restaurants.

Many Amish children attend a one-room schoolhouse from grades one to eight. Once they leave school, they spend time learning a trade so they can get a job and earn money to support themselves and their families.

Most Amish do not hold their worship services in a church building. They have church every other week, and it's held in the home, shop, or barn of different church members. In order to keep their religious beliefs, the Amish have chosen to live separate, plain lives.

Chapter 1

The Unforgettable Picnic

Boom!

Rachel Yoder shivered when the thunder clapped. She didn't like storms, and she especially didn't want one this evening. She was tempted to bite off the end of a fingernail like she often did when she felt nervous, but she caught herself in time. Nail biting could make you sick if your hands were dirty, and it was a bad habit she needed to break. Her mom often said so.

Rachel poked her head through the flap at the back of her family's dark gray Amish buggy and was glad to see that it wasn't raining. Maybe the storm would pass them and be on its way. Today was Friday, and this evening's picnic was her family's way to celebrate the last day of the school year. She didn't want anything to spoil their fun.

A horn honked from behind, and Pap guided their horse to the side of the road. Rachel peeked out the flap again, this time sticking her head out so she could get a good look at the fancy cars going by. *Woosh!* A gust of wind came up as she leaned out to wave at a shiny blue convertible. *Zip!* Rachel gasped as the white *kapp* she wore on her head sailed into the air and landed near the edge of the road. "*Ach!* My kapp—it's gonna get run over!" she hollered.

"Rachel Yoder, you know better than to lean out the buggy like that," Pap scolded. "What if you had fallen?"

"Can I get my kapp?" she asked tearfully.

"No!" Mom shook her head. "You might get hit by a car."

As the blue convertible started to pass, Rachel saw surprise on the face of the blond woman riding in the passenger's seat. The car pulled over behind their buggy, and the woman got out. She picked up Rachel's kapp and brought it over to the stopped buggy. "I believe this blew out of your buggy," she said, handing the limp-looking kapp to Rachel's father.

"Thank you," Pap said. "It belongs to my daughter."

"Thank you," Rachel echoed as Pap handed the kapp to her.

Rachel's cheeks heated with embarrassment as she put the kapp on her head.

"Stay in your seat now, Rachel," Pap said. He waited until the car had passed; then he pulled back into traffic.

Jacob, who was eleven, two years older than Rachel, sat up and yawned. He had been asleep in the seat beside her. "Are we there? I'm hungry."

"No, Pap stopped to let some cars go by." Rachel was careful not to mention that her kapp had blown off when she'd leaned out of the buggy. She knew Jacob would have teased her about it.

Jacob wrinkled his forehead, and the skin around his blue eyes crinkled. "Noisy cars sometimes scare our horse as they whiz by."

Rachel had seen horses do all kinds of strange things when they got spooked. She felt sorry for the horses. Still, she thought it would be fun to ride in a fast car. She leaned close to Jacob and whispered, "I saw a shiny blue convertible."

He shrugged. "So?"

"I'd like to ride in a car like that one someday," Rachel said. It was a secret she'd told no one else.

Jacob looked at Rachel as if she didn't have a lick of sense. Of course, she knew her brother thought most things she said and did were kind of strange.

"Don't you ever get tired of riding in this

closed-in buggy?" she asked.

"'Course not. I like our buggy just fine," he said.

"If I ever get the chance to ride in a convertible and see how fast it goes, I'm gonna take it," she mumbled.

Jacob nudged Rachel's arm. "You'd best not let anyone hear you speak such foolishness. It's one thing to ride in a car when we need to hire a driver for a reason, like to go to the big city. But just riding in one so you can see how fast it goes would be seen as a prideful, selfish wish."

Rachel crossed her arms and turned her back to her brother. She decided to drop the subject, but she turned around again and glared at Jacob when their parents weren't looking. He didn't understand the way she felt. He hardly ever did, and neither did their older brother, Henry. But at least Henry didn't act like something was wrong with her, the way Jacob did.

Boom! Rachel shuddered again. "It better not rain and spoil our picnic," she said, hoping Jacob wouldn't notice her hands shaking.

He elbowed her in the ribs. "What's the matter? Are you afraid of a little *dunner?*"

"It's not the thunder that makes me *naerfich*," she said, elbowing him right back. "It's those horrible bolts of *wedderleech* I'm worried about."

"We'll be okay. It's not even raining, so the storm will probably pass over us." Jacob leaned his head against the back of the seat and closed his eyes again.

Maybe if I think about something else I won't feel so nervous. Rachel glanced toward the front of the buggy, where her parents and older sister, Esther, sat chatting in the Pennsylvania Dutch language that Amish people often spoke.

"*Em Tom sei hutschle bin ich leedich,*" her father said.

Rachel clutched the folds in her dress. It worried her to hear Pap complaining about their horse Tom. Pap had just said, "I'm tired of Tom's neighing," and she wondered if he was planning to get rid of their old horse. Rachel couldn't bear the thought. Tom was a nice animal and had been their main buggy horse for many years. What was wrong with a little neighing? People talked whenever they wanted to say something. Shouldn't a horse be able to neigh whenever he felt like it?

Mom responded to Pap's comment, but another car whizzed past and drowned out her words. Rachel felt left out. She thought she should know if they planned to get rid of Tom.

"*Kens devun hot's duh kenne,*" Esther said.

Who was her sister talking about, and what

couldn't they do? Rachel was about to ask, but Pap pulled onto the dirt road leading to the pond, and she craned her neck to see the water.

"Yea! We're here, and the storm's passed by, so we can have our picnic!" Jacob jumped out of the buggy and ran toward the pond.

Esther stepped down next. The small white kapp perched on the back of her brown hair was always neatly in place. Not like Rachel's head covering, which often came loose during playtime.

Rachel climbed out of the buggy and reached up to touch her own kapp, to be sure it was still there. Mom often scolded her for not remembering to put it on when they went out in public.

Esther smiled. "It's a *wunderbaar gut* evening for a picnic."

"*Jah*," Mom said. "It *is* a wonderful good evening for a picnic. Too bad Henry didn't want to join us."

"He'd rather be with his *aldi*." Jacob rolled his eyes so they looked like they were crossed, and he coughed a couple of times as though he were gagging.

"Any sixteen-year-old boy who has a girlfriend wants to be with her. Henry thinks he's in love. That's what some nineteen-year-old girls think, too." Pap gave his brown beard a tug as he winked at Esther.

Esther's cheeks turned pink. Even though it hadn't been officially announced yet, Esther's family knew that she planned to marry Rudy King in the fall.

Rachel leaned into the buggy and grabbed a patchwork quilt from under the backseat. She didn't want to hear all this mushy love talk or think about getting married. She felt the best part of life was playing in the creek near their home, climbing a tree, or lying in the grass, dreaming about the interesting things she saw whenever they visited one of the nearby towns in Lancaster County, Pennsylvania.

Esther followed Rachel to a spot near the pond, and the two of them spread the quilt on the grass. Jacob ran along the water's edge, throwing flat rocks and hollering every time he made a perfect ripple. Pap unhitched Tom and tied him to a tree. Then he took their ice chest from the back of the buggy. Mom carried the picnic basket, and the two of them headed toward the quilt.

"I'm never getting married," Rachel told her sister.

Esther smoothed the edges of the quilt. "You'll change your mind someday."

"Rachel's probably right. She'll never get married 'cause she's too much of a *boppli*," Jacob said, as he joined them by the quilt.

"I am not a baby!"

"Are so."

Rachel couldn't let her brother have the last word, so she jerked the straw hat off his sandy-blond head and flung it into the air. "Am not!"

"Hey!" Jacob raced after his hat and grabbed it when it landed near the edge of the pond.

"Settle down, you two." Pap placed the ice chest on the grass. "We came to celebrate school being out, not to see who can shout the loudest or stir up the most trouble."

"That's right," Mom agreed as she opened the wicker basket and removed plates, cups, napkins, and silverware. "Let's put our energy into eating this good food that Esther and I prepared."

Rachel flopped onto the quilt with a groan. "What about me? I did the *blicking* of the peas for the salad."

"Do you want me to tell Mom how many you wasted by seeing if you could hit the goose's beak?" Jacob murmured quietly so their parents couldn't hear.

Rachel glared at him. She didn't think anyone had seen her. But the goose was always so mean to her, she couldn't resist the urge to *boing* a few peas at it.

Pap removed his hat and scooted over beside Rachel. "Shelling peas is important business."

Rachel smiled. At least someone appreciated her efforts. Her stomach rumbled as Esther opened the ice chest and set out the picnic food. Scents of golden brown fried chicken, tossed green salad with fresh peas, pickled beets, muffins with apple butter, and homemade root beer filled the air.

"It's surprising we had any root beer to bring on our picnic," Jacob said, nudging Rachel with his elbow. "If you'd dropped a few more jars the day Pap made the root beer, we wouldn't have any to drink."

Rachel frowned. She couldn't help it if she'd accidentally dropped two jars of root beer when she'd carried them to the cellar. They'd been slippery and didn't want to stay in her hands. Then she'd had a sticky mess to clean up.

"Clumsy butterfingers," Jacob taunted. "You're always making a mess."

"Am not."

"Are so."

"That's enough, you two," Mom said with a shake of her head.

Rachel settled back on the quilt. She couldn't wait to grab a drumstick and start eating. But first, all heads bowed for silent prayer. *Thank You, Lord, for this food and for the hands that prepared it,* she prayed. *Bless it to the needs of my body. Amen.*

When Pap cleared his throat, it signaled the end of prayer time. "Now let's eat until we're full!"

Mom passed the container of chicken to Rachel, and she reached for a drumstick. She added a spoonful of salad to her plate, two pickled beets, and a muffin. "Yum. Everything looks mighty gut." She was about to take a bite of the chicken, when Jacob smacked it right out of her hands. "Hey! That's mine!" she hollered.

"You want to eat that after a stinkbug's been on it?" he said, studying the leg.

"What?" Rachel eyed the chicken leg. Jacob was right. There was a fat old stinkbug on her piece of chicken.

Jacob smashed the bug with his thumb and handed it back to her. "Here you go."

A terrible odor drifted up to Rachel's nose. "Eww. . .that stinks! Why'd you do that, Jacob?"

He gave her a crooked grin. "Didn't figure you'd want to eat a stinkbug."

She put the chicken leg on the edge of her plate and pushed it away. "I'm not eating that stinky thing now."

Jacob snickered. "Jah, I'll bet that could make you real sick. You might even die from eating chicken that had a smelly bug like that on it."

"I'm not hungry now." Rachel folded her arms and frowned.

"Just take another piece of chicken and finish eating your meal," Mom said as she stared at Rachel over the top of her silver-framed glasses.

Pap looked over at Jacob and frowned. "You shouldn't be teasing your sister."

"Sorry," Jacob mumbled with his mouth full of muffin.

Rachel took another drumstick, and her stomach flip-flopped. What if she'd eaten that piece of chicken with the stinkbug on it? Could she have gotten sick? Her appetite was gone, but she knew if she didn't eat all her supper, she wouldn't get any dessert. She probably couldn't play after the meal, either. She bit into the fresh piece of chicken, trying not to think about the smelly stinkbug.

"I'm glad school's out," Jacob said. "I think we should have a picnic every night to celebrate."

Mom smiled. "We'll try to have several picnics this summer, but remember there's plenty of work to do. We women have a big garden to care for, and you'll help your *daed* and *bruder* in the fields."

"Right now I don't want to think about working." Jacob swiped a napkin across his face and jumped up. "I'm going to play in the pond."

"Don't get your clothes wet or muddy. I don't need dirty laundry to do when we get home," Mom said as Jacob sprinted off in his bare feet.

"Immer druwwle eiyets." Pap looked over at Mom and grinned.

"That's true, Levi," she responded. "There's always trouble somewhere. Especially when our two youngest children get so excited about summer that they start picking on each other."

Rachel didn't like the sound of that. She wasn't trouble—just curious, as her teacher would say.

She finished her dessert and scrambled to her feet. "I think I'll go wading, too."

Mom caught hold of Rachel's hand. "I hoped you and Esther would pick wild strawberries. Plenty are growing nearby, and they'd taste wunderbaar gut for breakfast tomorrow."

"Do I have to pick berries?" Rachel whined. "I want to play in the water."

"Do as your *mamm* asks." Pap's eyebrows furrowed, and Rachel knew he meant what he said.

Esther stood and smoothed the wrinkles from her long blue dress. She looked at Rachel and smiled. "I can pick the berries on my own."

While Rachel waited for her mother's reply, an irritating bee buzzed overhead.

"I guess it would be okay," Mom finally agreed.

Rachel swatted at the bee. Big mistake. A few seconds later, a burning pain shot from her finger all the way up her arm.

"Ach!" she cried, jumping up and down from the shock of the bee's sting. She shook her finger and waved her arm.

"Calm down," Pap instructed as he took a look at her hand. "Scoot over to the pond, take a little dirt and water, then pat the mud on the stinger. That should help draw it out."

Rachel dashed to the pond. She had wanted to go there, but not with a cruel bee stinger making her whole arm throb.

Near the water's edge, she found Jacob building a dam from mud, rocks, and twigs. His dark trousers, held up by tan suspenders, were rolled up to his knees.

He gets to have all the fun! Rachel thought. *It's not fair.*

She scooped some dirt into her hand and added several drops of water. When a muddy paste formed, she spread it on her sore finger. Soon the throbbing lessened, so Rachel decided to see if she could make a better dam than Jacob's.

She waded into the cool water and giggled as it splashed against her legs. The bottom was mushy and squished between her bare toes.

"You'd better watch out," Jacob warned. "Your dress is getting wet."

Rachel glanced down. Sure enough, the hem was dark from where the water had soaked through. "I wish I didn't have to wear long dresses all the time," she grumbled. "You're lucky to be a boy."

Jacob frowned as if Rachel had said something terrible. "You complain too much. Can't you be happy with the way things are?"

Rachel stuck her finger between her teeth and bit off the end of the nail, spitting it into the water. "Sometimes I wonder if I'm supposed to be Amish."

Her brother's eyebrows lifted. "You were *born* Amish."

"I know, but sometimes I feel—" Rachel stared into space. Way down inside, where she hid her deepest secrets, she wondered what it would be like if she could do some of the things the non-Amish children her people called "English" got to do. "Sometimes I wish I could wear pants and shirts like the English girls do," she said.

"Sisters! Who can figure 'em out?" Jacob pointed at Rachel. "Especially you, little *bensel.*"

"I am not a silly child. If anyone's silly, it's you." Rachel flicked some water in Jacob's direction, and the drops landed on his shirtsleeve, making little dark circles.

Her brother only chuckled as he kept building his mud dam.

Rachel plodded toward the shore and gathered a few more twigs. She would make her dam even bigger than Jacob's, and then he would see that she wasn't a bensel. "Now, what did I do with that twig I was going to use?" she muttered.

"It's in your hand, little bensel."

Rachel's face flushed. She was about to say something, when Mom called, "Rachel! Jacob! Come dry your feet. It's time to go."

Jacob cupped his hands around his mouth. "Coming!" he shouted.

When her brother hurried away, Rachel bent down, placed the twig and another clump of mud on the side of her dam, and stepped back to admire her work. Suddenly, her foot slipped on a slimy rock, and she stumbled. She swayed back and forth for a moment, then *splash!* Rachel landed facedown in the water.

She was still sputtering and trying to stand in the slippery mud when Pap reached her. He scooped her into his strong arms, and Rachel leaned against his shoulder. "I didn't mean to fall in the water," she sobbed.

"You should have come when your mamm called," Pap said harshly, as he tromped up the grassy bank and placed Rachel on the ground near the horse and buggy.

She stood dripping wet, with her teeth chattering. Her kapp had come off and hung around her neck by its narrow ties, and most of her hair had come loose from the bun at the back of her head. She didn't know whether to laugh or cry.

Jacob pointed at Rachel and howled. "Your hair's stickin' out in all directions. You look like a prickly blond porcupine."

"Do not!" Rachel snapped. She knew she might look silly, but she didn't look like a prickly porcupine.

Mom wrapped the picnic quilt around Rachel's shoulders.

"I'm sorry, Mom." Rachel sniffed and swiped at the water dripping from her soggy hair onto her cheeks. She wiped her muddy face, arms, and legs on the quilt.

"Sorry is good, but if you'd come when you were called, you probably wouldn't have fallen into the water," Mom said crossly, looking at the muddy prints Rachel had left on the quilt. "When we get home, you'll have laundry to do."

Rachel frowned. She hadn't meant to get her

clothes wet. Why should she have to wash them? After all, the quilt was an old one; that's why they'd taken it on the picnic.

"We'd better head for home," Pap said. He helped the women into the buggy, and Jacob scrambled in after them.

The ride home was not pleasant. Rachel's wet dress stuck to her skin like tape. Shifting on the hard seat, she felt a shiver tickle her spine, and she pulled the quilt tightly around her shoulders.

Jumbled thoughts skittered through Rachel's mind. Jacob thought she was silly, and she knew she'd caused trouble for her parents. She wondered if every day of summer would be as topsy-turvy as this picnic day. She decided she'd better steer clear of trouble!

Chapter 2

Afraid of the Dark

The sun was just beginning to show when Rachel came downstairs for breakfast the next morning. She knew her mother would be up early, getting ready to go to the Millers' house. Mom planned to help Anna Miller do some cleaning in preparation to host the biweekly Sunday worship service at the Millers' house in two days. Since Rachel was eager to call on their neighbors, she found it easier to get out of bed so early.

Rachel took an apple-crumb pie out of the refrigerator and placed it on the table. It was one of her favorite breakfast pies, and her stomach growled as she thought of how good it would taste.

"When breakfast is over, we'll need to hurry through our chores," Mom said. "Esther's already milking the cows. Henry and Pap are hitching the horse to our buggy, and I sent Jacob to the henhouse to gather eggs."

Rachel snickered. "Jacob always says that gathering eggs is women's work. He must be really *gretzich* this morning."

"I don't care if Jacob is crabby. If he thinks only women can gather eggs, he's sorely mistaken. That kind of thinking is just plain foolish." Mom reached for the kettle of oatmeal sitting near the back of the stove. She pushed a wisp of pale blond hair away from her face, where it had worked its way out from under the kapp covering her bun.

Rachel had just finished setting the table when the rest of the family came into the kitchen. Everyone gathered around the table and bowed their heads for silent prayer. Rachel prayed that she would be allowed to have two pieces of apple-crumb pie and also that she'd have lots of fun at the Millers'.

By nine o'clock, breakfast was over, the kitchen had been cleaned, and Mom and Rachel had finished the rest of their chores. Satisfied and full after eating a bowl of oatmeal and two pieces of pie, Rachel followed Mom outside and climbed into their buggy. She felt certain that today would turn out better than yesterday.

"Are you sure you won't come with us to the

Millers'?" Mom asked Esther, who stood in front of the buggy, stroking the horse's ear.

Esther shook her head and smiled sweetly. "Rudy is picking me up soon. We're going to the Hertzlers' place to look at some horses. He's thinking about buying a new one."

Mom nodded and handed Rachel her kapp. "I found this hanging on the wall peg in the kitchen. Were you planning to go without it, or were you daydreaming again?"

With a sigh, Rachel put the head covering in place. "Sorry, Mom. I forgot."

"You've been so forgetful lately," Mom said. "What seems to be the problem?"

Rachel shrugged. "I've got a lot on my mind." After all, school was out now, and she had lots of plans for her summer.

Mom gave Rachel a curious look but made no reply. She turned to wave at Esther and started the horse trotting down the lane leading to the main road.

"Sure was a nice picnic supper we had yesterday, jah?" Mom said as they rode along.

"Except for when I almost ate a stinkbug, got stung by a bee, and fell in the pond," Rachel mumbled.

Mom reached over to touch Rachel's hand.

"The stinkbug wasn't such a big thing. The bee sting was an accident. And if you had come out of the water when you were called, you might not have fallen in."

"I was just trying to have a little fun."

"I know, but you must learn to listen. That will help you stay out of trouble."

Rachel nodded. "I've been wondering. . . ," she said, changing the subject.

"What's that?"

"Yesterday on the way to the pond, I heard Pap say something about Tom neighing too much."

"That horse seems to complain about everything these days," Mom said with a click of her tongue.

Rachel's forehead wrinkled with concern. Tom was getting old and couldn't do everything he used to do. Maybe he had a right to complain.

They soon turned onto a gravel driveway. Howard and Anna Miller's three-story house was even larger than the Yoders' home. The Miller family included six boys and four girls—so they needed lots of room. Two of the girls were already married and lived with their husbands on their own farms, but the rest of the Miller children still lived at home.

As soon as Rachel climbed down from the

buggy, she spotted Anna Miller chopping weeds in the garden. Her plump figure was bent over a row of strawberry plants. Beside her stood six-year-old Katie. Nearby sat little Sarah's baby carriage. When Anna saw Rachel and her mother, she waved and set her garden hoe aside.

Mom and Anna greeted each other in the Pennsylvania Dutch language, while Rachel squatted next to the carriage so she could see the baby better. "Sarah sure is a pretty boppli," she said.

"Jah, we think she's a pretty baby, too," Anna replied with a smile.

For the next several minutes, Anna, Mom, Rachel, and Katie admired the infant and made silly baby sounds.

"I expect we should get busy with the cleaning and baking," Mom finally said.

Anna nodded. "I appreciate you coming to help today, Miriam. Since the boppli came, I seem to be getting further behind on all my chores."

While Mom helped Anna clean house, Rachel looked after Katie and baby Sarah. She liked being in charge of the little ones. It made her feel important. Besides, Mom had promised Rachel some free time after lunch, and she looked forward to exploring the Millers' yard.

"Let's go look for the *busslin* that my cat, Missy, had," Katie suggested.

She pointed to a little hole under the front porch. "They could be in there."

Rachel parked the baby carriage under the shade of a maple tree. Then she and Katie knelt and peered into the opening.

"I don't see any kittens," Rachel said as she stuck her hand inside the hole and felt all around. When she pulled her hand out again, she discovered a grasshopper perched on the end of her thumb.

Katie squealed and jumped away. "Eww! I don't like bugs!"

Rachel set the grasshopper in the flower bed. "I think bugs are okay as long as they're not on my food."

"Let's go see if the kittens are in the barn," Katie said, tugging Rachel's hand.

Rachel pushed the baby carriage down the dirt path. When she and Katie entered the barn, she parked the carriage near some bales of hay stacked by the door. Then Katie looked for the kittens inside an empty horse stall while Rachel climbed the hayloft to hunt for them there.

"Ahhhh!"

Rachel's heart lurched as she heard the shrill scream. She scrambled down the ladder. Katie stood on a bale of hay, trembling from head to toe.

"What's wrong, Katie? Why are you standing up there?"

Katie pointed across the room. "*Maus*. I saw a maus."

Rachel could hardly believe anyone would be afraid of a little old mouse. She thought mice were cute. And mice didn't chase you around, nipping at your legs, the way their old goose sometimes did.

"The maus won't hurt you," she said, holding her hand out to Katie. "Come on, let's go outside and swing."

Katie nodded, and pushing the baby carriage, the two girls headed behind the barn. Rachel loved to swing—and it was hard for her to take turns. But while Katie swung, Rachel pushed Sarah in her carriage so she wouldn't fuss. Then when it was Rachel's turn to swing, Katie pushed her sister's carriage around in the grass.

At noon, the dinner bell rang. Rachel and Katie rushed into the house, where everyone took turns washing up at the sink. Finally each person was seated at the huge wooden table in the center of the Millers' kitchen. Howard Miller and his six sons ate quickly so they could get back to the fields to work more, but Rachel took her time eating. She enjoyed every bite of the tasty cold meats and cheeses, homemade bread, potato salad, canned applesauce, and chewy peanut butter cookies Anna had served for lunch. Anna and Mom had already begun to clear away the dishes when Rachel swallowed her last bite.

"I'm going to put my *kinner* down for a nap so we can finish our cleaning without any interruptions," Anna said to Mom as she scooted Katie toward the stairs. "If there's time, maybe we can do some baking this afternoon."

Rachel was glad she didn't have to take a nap like the younger children. She helped her mother wash the dishes. When they had been dried and put away, she asked if she could go outside to play.

"Jah, but don't get into any trouble," Mom said, peering at Rachel over the top of her glasses.

"I won't. I promise."

As soon as Rachel opened the back door and stepped onto the porch, she noticed that the sky was filled with heavy, gray clouds. The air smelled like rain, and she drew in a deep breath. She slipped off her shoes, hopped down the porch steps, and skipped across the lawn.

Her first stop was Anna's flower garden. Rachel loved flowers, and she fought the urge to pick a few of the prettiest ones, since she hadn't asked for permission. Besides, too many bees landed on the flowers, and Rachel didn't want to get stung again.

Rachel headed down the path that led to the creek. Howard Miller's waterwheel squeaked as it turned, making the water ripple and gurgle. Rachel knew the wheel was important because it created some of the power used on the Millers' farm. Because electricity was considered worldly, the Amish in her area used other methods of energy that weren't so modern.

While Rachel tossed rocks into the creek, a gust of wind rustled the treetops, and a few drops of rain splashed to the ground. She shivered at first, worried she might be caught in a storm. Then she smiled. If it rained hard enough, there might be some mud puddles she could tromp through. Meanwhile, she would go play in the barn. She was only halfway to the barn when she saw Katie's cat, Missy, run out the open barn door, followed by four little gray and white kittens. *They must have been in there the whole time and we missed them,* she thought.

Rachel called to Missy, but the cat ignored her and kept running. Thunder boomed, and all five cats raced down the steps and through the open doorway of the underground root cellar. The wind blew so hard Rachel had to hold on to her kapp in order to keep it from blowing off her head.

She hurried after the cats. As she stumbled

down the stairs and into the small, cold room, she shivered. Even with the door open, it was dark inside, and she didn't see any sign of Missy or her kittens.

Rachel blinked a couple of times. As her eyes adjusted to the darkness, she noticed wooden shelves fastened to the wall. They held glass jars filled with home-canned fruits and vegetables. Empty boxes sat on the concrete floor, waiting for the crops of potatoes, carrots, and other root vegetables the Millers would harvest later.

"Here, kitty, kitty," Rachel called. Neither Missy nor any of her kittens responded. Rachel only heard the howling wind and steady raindrops splattering on the steps outside the cellar door.

More thunder rumbled, followed by another gust of wind.

Bam! The cellar door slammed shut, and Rachel screamed as the darkness swallowed her.

Rachel wasn't afraid of much, but two things really frightened her—dark places and thunderstorms. She had taken a risk by coming into the dark cellar. Now she had to be brave and deal with both of the things that scared her most.

Rachel drew in a shaky breath, then inched her way forward. When her fingers touched the doorknob, she turned it and pushed the door.

Nothing happened. Leaning her weight against the heavy wooden door, Rachel pushed and pushed until she had no strength left in her arms. Her heart pounded like a woodpecker tapping on a tree. "I'm trapped! I'm afraid. . .and nobody knows I'm down here."

Rachel pressed her cheek to the door. "Someone, please help me!"

Plinkety plink. Plinkety plink. No answer except the rain hitting the door.

She stuck her finger in her mouth and gnawed off a fingernail. She tried to pray, but her words came out all jumbled. "Wh–what if they—" *Sniff.* "N–never find me?" *Sniff. Sniff.* "H–help me, Lord."

Rachel remembered hearing a minister at church once say that heaven has no dark places. That was a comforting thought, but it didn't help the situation she faced right now.

Something soft and furry rubbed against Rachel's ankle, and she knew it was one of Missy's kittens. She bent to pick it up, and the soft ball of fur purred when she lifted it to her face. Then it licked Rachel's nose with its rough, wet tongue.

Rachel dropped to her knees, and as she touched each lump of fur climbing into her lap, she realized that all four kittens and Missy were there.

She felt a little better knowing she wasn't alone, but she was still afraid. *There must be an oil lamp down here,* she thought. *I just need to find it.*

Rachel gently pushed the cats aside and stood shakily. She felt her way around the room until her hand touched something cold and hard. "It's a lantern!" she exclaimed. Her fingers moved up and down, back and forth along the shelf that held the lantern until she touched a book of matches. With a sigh of relief, she picked it up, struck a match, and lit the lantern. A warm glow spread throughout the tiny room, showing the shelves full of canning jars.

Rachel spotted a jar of pickled beets, and her stomach rumbled. It must be near suppertime. Would Mom go home without her? After all, she'd told Rachel to stay out of trouble, and here Rachel was now, in the middle of disaster.

"Maybe I should have a little snack—just in case," she murmured. "Anna probably won't miss a few beets from one jar, and I'm sure she wouldn't want me to starve to death."

Rachel picked up the old-fashioned glass jar, pulled the heavy wire off the top, and popped off the lid. She loved beets, especially when they were pickled with vinegar, sugar, and cinnamon. "Mmm. . .they smell so good." She poked two fingers inside, withdrew one spicy red beet, and popped it into her mouth.

"Yum."

As Rachel started back across the room, a kitten darted in front of her, and she stumbled. The jar crashed to the floor, breaking the glass and splattering beets and sticky red juice everywhere. The juice even dotted the kittens' fur and Rachel's dress. "Ach, what have I done?" she moaned.

She knew beet juice stained clothes. Her mother wouldn't be happy about trying to get the red splotches out of Rachel's dress. She hoped the Millers wouldn't be upset about having a stained floor.

Suddenly, the room went dark again. Rachel had noticed that the oil was low in the lamp, but she didn't expect it to go out *this* soon. Rachel held very still, remembering that she wasn't wearing any shoes and that glass covered the floor.

Unsure of what else to do, Rachel carefully touched the floor to make sure no glass was in her way as she dropped to her knees. She prayed, "Dear God, You know I'm afraid of the dark, so would You please help me not cry?"

Just like before, the kittens and the mother cat hopped into Rachel's lap, which made her feel less afraid. She closed her eyes, leaned her head against the cellar door, and was soon fast asleep.

Chapter 3

A Wunderbaar Surprise

Rachel was dreaming about pickled beets, kittens, and shiny blue cars, when the cellar door jerked open, and she fell backward. She sat up, feeling dazed, and looked over her shoulder. She saw Howard Miller and his sons Jake and Martin, each holding a lantern.

"The little bensel got herself locked in the cellar." Jake chuckled and slapped his knee.

Rachel didn't see what was so funny, and she didn't like being called a silly child any more now than when Jacob had called her that. "What time is it?" she asked with a yawn. "How long have I been down here?"

"It's half past six," Howard answered. "Your mamm has been frantic with worry. She said she'd planned to head for home by five o'clock, but when she couldn't find you, she sent me and the boys out looking."

"I followed Missy and her busslin into the cellar. Then the wind blew the door shut, and I couldn't open it again." Rachel bit her bottom lip to keep it from quivering. "I—I didn't know if anyone would ever find me."

"Aw, sure they would," Martin said with a snicker. "Come winter, when Mom needed some of her canned food, she would have headed straight to the cellar. What a surprise she would have found in here, too!"

Rachel knew Martin was only teasing, but she wasn't amused.

Jake sent a beam of light from his lantern all around the room and made a sweeping gesture with his other hand. "What's all this mess with the broken glass and the beet juice?"

"I—I was hungry, and I—" Rachel's voice broke, and she drew in a deep breath to get control of her emotions. "I know I shouldn't have taken the beets without asking, and I'm sorry about the mess. If you'll leave one of your lanterns here so I can see, I'll clean it up."

"Never mind, Rachel. I'll see that everything is taken care of later on." Howard patted Rachel's head. "I'm glad you've been found. Now we'd best get you back to the house so your mamm can quit worrying."

Rachel pointed to the kittens that lay curled in a ball next to their mother. "What about them? We can't leave Missy and her little busslin alone in the cellar."

"The door's open now, so they can leave whenever they want." Howard nodded at his sons. "Hurry to the house and tell Rachel's mother that we found her."

Jake and Martin took off on a run, and Howard scooped Rachel into his strong arms. She felt safe and secure and so relieved that she had been found. She was glad he'd been so nice about the mess she'd made.

Later that evening, after Rachel had bathed and changed into clean clothes, she sat with her family around the supper table, telling them how she had been trapped in the cellar. "And I only had the company of Missy and her four little busslin," she said at the end of the story.

Mom handed Rachel a glass of cold milk, and Pap passed her a basket of warm bread. "You had quite an ordeal today," he said. "Did you learn anything from it?"

Rachel nodded. "I'll never go into another root

cellar without telling someone where I'm going."
She didn't mention how scared she had been.

"God was watching over you today," Mom said,
as she helped herself to some meatloaf and handed
the platter to Esther.

"He was?" Rachel asked as she bit into a piece
of bread.

"Sure," Mom replied. "God sent Missy and her
busslin to be with you in the cellar."

"Was it dark in the cellar?" Esther asked as she
passed the platter to Rachel.

"Most of the time it was." Rachel drank some
of her milk. "I was worried that the kittens would
be afraid of the dark, so I found an oil lamp and a
book of matches. The cellar was well lit until the
lamp ran out of oil."

"Like those furry critters needed any light," her
oldest brother, Henry, put in.

Jacob snickered. "I'll bet Rachel was the real
scaredy-cat."

Rachel wasn't about to tell her brothers how
frightened she had been, but before she could say
anything more, Pap gave Jacob a stern look. Rachel
figured she would get one of those looks if she
said anything unkind to her brother, so she crossed
her eyes and wrinkled her nose at him when her
parents weren't looking.

Jacob crossed his eyes and wrinkled his nose right back at her. Then he grabbed a hunk of meatloaf and popped a piece into his mouth.

"Did you get everything done at the Millers' today?" Esther asked, looking at Mom.

"We finished the cleaning," Mom said. "But when the rain started, I decided that Rachel and I should go home, so Anna and I never did any baking." She glanced over at Rachel. "When the wind started howling like crazy, I thought you would hurry back to the house."

Rachel said nothing. She just stared at the blob of spinach Pap had put on her plate. Then she reached for the bowl of mashed potatoes, added a scoop to her plate, and stirred the ugly, green, slimy-looking blob in with the potatoes. Spinach was her least favorite vegetable, and she hoped if she mixed it with the potatoes, the yucky stuff might go down a little easier.

"When the dunner and wedderleech started and you still didn't return to the house, I began to worry." Mom reached past Esther and patted Rachel's hand as Rachel was about to take a bite of her mashed potatoes. The spoon flipped out of her hand, and the gooey glob flew across the table and landed on Jacob's plate, spattering the blob of slimy spinach and potatoes all over the front of his shirt.

"Ugh!" Jacob scowled at Rachel. "You did that on purpose, Rachel-the-scaredy-cat, who's afraid of thunder and lightning."

"Did not."

"Did so."

"Did not."

"Did—"

"That's enough!" Pap clapped his hands, and Rachel and Jacob stopped arguing.

Rachel knew better than to act like this at the table, but Jacob made her so angry she could hardly control her temper. *I know God loves everyone,* she thought, *but I'm guessing Jacob tries the Lord's patience as much as he does mine.*

Mom pointed to the sink. "Jacob, you had better get that mess cleaned off your shirt before it leaves a stain. I've had enough dirty clothes to deal with for one day."

Rachel knew her mother was talking about the dress stained with beet juice that she had worn to the Millers'. She figured no matter how much Mom scrubbed that dress, the ugly red stains would probably never come out.

Jacob glared at Rachel and pushed away from the table with a groan. He marched across the room, opened the cupboard door under the sink, and dumped Rachel's potato-spinach mess into the garbage can. Then he wet a dishrag and started rubbing the front of his shirt real hard.

Mom passed the bowl of spinach to Esther, who handed it to Rachel.

Rachel knew she would be in trouble if she didn't take some, so she dipped the spoon in and plucked out a tiny piece, placing it on the edge of her plate.

Mom clicked her tongue, and Pap raised his dark, bushy eyebrows. Rachel added a little larger piece and felt relieved when Pap nodded and said, "Jah, okay."

"How did the Millers know where to look for you?" Henry asked, as Rachel held her nose, popped the spinach into her mouth, and washed it down with a gulp of milk.

"Howard sent two of his boys to look down by the creek," Mom said before Rachel could reply. "Two of his sons went to their neighbor's place to see if Rachel had gone there, while Jake, Martin, and Howard searched their own farm. When they had looked in all the obvious places, Howard decided to try the root cellar. I'm glad they found you before we got the whole neighborhood in an uproar."

Rachel sighed, remembering how scared she had been during most of the ordeal. "I'm glad he thought to look there. I wondered if I would ever get out of that terrible place."

Just as Jacob was about to sit down again, someone knocked on the back door. "I'll get it!" Jacob raced across the room and flung the door open.

Esther's boyfriend, Rudy, entered the kitchen. He carried a wicker basket draped with a piece of green cloth. "Sorry to disturb your supper," he said, glancing at the table.

"That's all right. Would you like to join us?" Mom asked.

"No, thanks. I stopped at the Millers' place this evening to drop off benches for our church service on Sunday. Howard asked me to deliver this special surprise to Rachel." He smiled and stepped toward the table, holding the basket in front of him.

Pap nodded at Rachel. "Why don't you see what it is?"

Rachel didn't have to be asked twice. She loved surprises.

Rudy handed her the basket, and when she lifted the cloth, she gasped. "Oh, it's one of Missy's busslin!" She stroked the kitten's head. "I'm going to call you Cuddles."

Esther's eyebrows rose. "Cuddles?"

Rachel nodded. "All of the busslin were so

cuddly when they kept me company in the cold, dark cellar."

"Howard told me about your ordeal. He said you seemed worried about the kittens," Rudy said. "He wanted you to have one of them, and this is the *bussli* he chose for you."

The gray and white kitten, with a speck of red beet juice still on one paw, nestled against Rachel's arm and purred. Rachel leaned over and nuzzled its wet nose. "Can I keep her?" she asked, looking at Mom and then at Pap.

Mom smiled. "If it's all right with your daed, it's fine by me."

Pap tugged on the end of his beard. "I suppose it'll be okay, but you must promise to take care of it."

"And the bussli will sleep in the barn with all the other animals," Mom quickly added.

Rachel placed the kitten on the floor and ran to the table to give Mom and Pap a hug and a kiss on the cheek. "This is such a wunderbaar surprise! I promise I'll take good care of Cuddles."

Jacob groaned and shook his head. "What a dumb name for a cat."

Rachel hurried back to the kitten and lifted it into her arms. "It's not dumb. You're just saying that because you're jealous."

"Am not. You should name it Trouble since

that's all you ever get into."

Rachel didn't feel like arguing with Jacob anymore. And she didn't want to think of the trouble she'd caused that day for her mother and the Millers. She felt happy to be holding one of the sweet little bundles of fur that had snuggled in her lap and kept her company while she was trapped in the cellar.

Chapter 4

Egg Yolks and Hopping Frogs

Rachel carefully opened her eyes. She squinted at the ray of sunlight streaming through a tiny hole in the dark shade covering her bedroom window. It was time to get up and do her morning chores. Then she and her family would go to the three-hour church service at Howard and Anna Miller's house.

Rachel yawned and sat up. Swinging her legs over the side of the bed, she stood and hurried to the other side of the room. The dress and apron she usually wore to do her chores hung on a wall peg near her dressing table. She took them down and quickly dressed.

When Rachel entered the kitchen, she saw her mother standing at the counter, cutting a shoofly pie into equal pieces. "Hurry and do your chores,"

Mom said. "We don't want to be late for church."
She handed Rachel a wicker basket. "Be sure to go
out to the chicken coop first. I'm scrambling eggs
for breakfast and need a few more."

Rachel grabbed the basket and rushed out of
the house. She paused at the barn door, tempted
to play with Cuddles, who had been made to sleep
in the barn because that's where Mom thought
animals belonged. Rachel peeked in and saw
Cuddles sleeping on a bale of hay, so she hurried
on to the chicken coop, knowing she could play
with the kitten later.

Inside the chicken coop, Rachel found four
empty nests and six more with hens sitting in
them. She hoped there were eggs under those hens,
because she didn't want to return to the house
empty-handed.

Rachel placed the basket on the floor and
picked up the first chicken. *Bawk! Bawk!* The red
hen fussed, but Rachel didn't give in. She had a job
to do, and she planned to get it done.

Three eggs were in that nest, so Rachel leaned
down and placed them inside the basket.

Bawk! Bawk! The hen hopped into the basket
and fluffed up her feathers like she belonged there.

"That is not your nest," Rachel scolded,
nudging the chicken with the toe of her sneaker.

Usually Rachel came out to the coop in her bare feet, but she'd had a bath last night and didn't want to get anything grimy or slimy between her toes.

With another blaring squawk, the hen hopped out of the basket and waddled to the other side of the coop. Rachel hurried down the line, removing each hen from its nest and filling her basket with their bulky brown eggs. When she was done, she left the coop and headed across the yard toward the house.

Rachel had only gone as far as the clothesline when she noticed a couple of fat green frogs hopping along the edge of the grass near the garden.

If I could take the two of them with me, I could race them after church, she thought.

Rachel set the basket of eggs on the ground and ran to the barn for a small box. When she returned, the frogs were gone. She walked up and down the garden rows and finally found them under the leaves of a strawberry plant.

Rachel dropped to her knees, inched forward, and reached out her hand. One frog hopped to the left. The other frog hopped to the right. She gritted her teeth, determined to catch both of those leaping frogs.

Rachel crawled slowly until she spotted one

of the frogs again. She lifted her hand, held her breath—then, quick as wink, she grabbed it. The other frog hopped out of the garden, so Rachel hurried and put the first frog in the box. Then she snapped the cardboard flaps down fast. Next, Rachel followed the second frog as it hopped across the grass and into one of Mom's flower beds. It took her three tries to catch it, as the frog hopped away every time her hand came near, but she finally captured the critter and put it in the box along with its friend.

Rachel ran to the buggy, which had already been hitched to old Tom. She opened the back door and slipped the box under the backseat.

Remembering the eggs she'd been sent to gather, Rachel rushed back to the spot where she had left the basket. She bent over to pick it up and had taken only a few steps when she heard a shrill, *Honk! Honk!*

Rachel whirled around and gasped when she saw Clara the goose heading straight for her. Rachel knew it wasn't right to hate any animal, but she certainly didn't like Clara—at all. And Clara didn't like her. Any time Clara saw Rachel, she made a beeline for her. If Clara caught up with Rachel, she'd nip at Rachel, a goose's way of biting. Goose bites, Rachel had learned, hurt very much.

"Shoo! Shoo!" Rachel cried. She clung to the basket with one hand and waved her other hand at the honking bird, but Clara kept coming.

Rachel screamed and ran for the house as fast as she could. She was almost to the porch when she felt Clara's *nip! nip!* on the backs of her legs.

"Ouch!" Tears stung Rachel's eyes as she tried to hop out of the goose's reach. She grabbed the railing and pulled herself forward. Missing the first step, she tripped and fell.

When Rachel picked herself up she noticed the basket of eggs. "Oh, no, they're all broken, and now I'm a mess!" Runny, yellow yolks mixed with pieces of shell and the slimy white part of the eggs clung to the front of her apron. She whirled around, prepared to give Clara the chase of her life, but the goose was gone.

"Always trouble somewhere," Rachel grumbled, as she trudged into the house. She wasn't looking forward to telling her mother that they would have no more eggs for breakfast.

To Rachel's surprise, Mom didn't scold her about the broken eggs. She only said, "I told your daed he should get rid of that mean old goose. One of these days, she'll end up in my stewing pot." Then Mom said she would just use the eggs she already had and might fix a batch of oatmeal to go with them.

"Guess I'd better go upstairs and change into my church dress," Rachel said.

Mom nodded. "I'll need to tend those wounds the goose put on your legs, too."

"I can do it." Rachel felt better now that she was safely away from Clara.

An hour later, the Yoder family pulled into the Millers' yard. Rachel noticed several other Amish buggies lined up next to Howard Miller's barn. She leaned close to Jacob and whispered, "I hope Cousin Mary is here today. I can't wait to tell her about Cuddles."

Jacob tugged on Rachel's sleeve. "I still say that's a dumb name for a cat."

She jerked her arm away. "And I say it's not." She hardly noticed that their buggy had stopped.

"It's a bensel name!" Jacob taunted.

"You're a bensel!" Rachel accused, her voice rising.

"Rachel!" Pap's voice interrupted the squabble.

Rachel looked at her parents' horrified faces. Then she realized Pap had parked their buggy next to Bishop Wagler's buggy. Bishop Wagler was the head minister of their church, and she always felt a little nervous when he was around.

The bishop had stepped to their buggy to greet Pap, and she wondered if he'd heard her and Jacob arguing. He pulled his fingers through the ends of his long, gray beard and greeted Pap in Pennsylvania Dutch.

Pap turned to respond to him and climbed down from the buggy, but Mom sat there, frowning at Rachel. Rachel gulped. She knew Mom felt misbehaving in public was one of the worst things a child could do. To behave badly in front of the minister was even worse.

"You're going to get it now!" Jacob whispered to her as they climbed out of the buggy.

"But you started it!" she hissed at him.

"Um-hmm." Rachel heard her mother clear her voice as a warning.

As soon as Pap had unhitched the horse and put it in the Millers' corral with the other horses, he, Henry, and Jacob joined other men and boys under a leafy maple tree. Mom and Esther joined the women, who stood on the front porch visiting. Rachel grabbed her frog box and hurried to look for her cousin. By the time she found Mary standing near the barn, she had no time to tell Mary about the frog race. Most of the people were moving indoors so church could begin.

Rachel put the box with the frogs on the Millers' porch, next to the kitchen. Then she hurried into the living room to sit on a long wooden bench on the women's side of the room.

Mom and Esther sat near Mary's mother, Irma, and Rachel and Mary sat on a bench ahead of them with some other girls their age. Pap, Henry, and Jacob took their seats on the men's side of the room.

Deacon Byler passed out the hymnals. While the congregation sang, the bishop and the other two ministers left the room. Rachel knew they always left the service during this time to discuss church business and decide who would preach the first sermon. Rachel hoped Bishop Wagler hadn't heard her and Jacob arguing, and she worried that Mom would punish her when they got home. Of course, Jacob had been in on the argument, so he should be punished, too.

Rachel shot a glance at her mother. Mom smiled and sang with all her heart. Tears threatened to squeeze from Rachel's eyes. If the bishop said anything to Mom or Pap about how disagreeable Rachel was, Rachel knew her parents would feel a terrible shame.

She didn't know any other children who seemed to get into as much trouble as she did!

When the church leaders returned, the singing ended. Rachel leaned close to Mary and whispered, "I have some news to tell you."

"Really, what is it?"

"I got a special surprise Friday night. And that's not all. Today I brought along a couple of—"

"Um-hmm." Rachel heard Mom quietly clearing her throat.

When Rachel looked over her shoulder, she saw Mom put a finger to her lips and give Rachel a stern look over the top of her glasses. "Shh. . ."

Rachel knew she was expected to be quiet during church, but it was so hard to sit still and not talk. She was already in trouble for squabbling with Jacob in front of the bishop, so she knew she'd better do as Mom said.

Halfway through the service, Anna Miller slipped out of the room. She quickly returned with a platter of dried apple pieces. She gave some to the children so they could sit through the rest of the service without getting too hungry.

Rachel ate hers eagerly, thinking about the noon meal and the time of fellowship afterward. She had just finished the last bite when she heard a strange noise.

Ribbet! Ribbet!

Rachel looked down. *Oh, no!* One of the frogs leaped along the floor under the bench in front of her. She held her breath, praying no one would notice. She hoped the frog might hop toward her so she could capture it.

The sermon had just ended, and the people were about to sing a closing hymn, when the frog jumped with all its might. It landed in the lap of Sarah King, an elderly woman sitting directly in front of Rachel.

"Ahhhh!" Sarah screeched. She jumped off her bench, knocking the frog to the floor. It sat dazed for a moment. Then it hopped in one direction and then another.

Jacob jumped up and dashed across the aisle. He tried to capture the frog, but the sly old critter kept hopping away. Martin Miller joined the chase as shrieks and hollers came from all sides of the room. But the frog continued to jump, and the boys, wearing determined expressions, kept darting after it.

Rachel gasped when the frog landed in ten-year-old Elsie Byler's lap. Elsie screamed and jumped up. Everyone sitting on her bench jumped up, too.

Jacob raced across the room, took a flying leap, missed the frog, and knocked over the bench.

Ribbet! Ribbet! The frog leaped again; this time Jacob grabbed it, but it leaped out of his hands and landed on seven-year-old Aaron King's shoulder. Then before anyone could move, it hopped down the boy's shirt.

Aaron hollered and raced around the room as if he'd been stung by a bee. Aaron's mother reached out as her son ran by. She pulled the back of his shirt out of his trousers. The frog sailed through the air, landing near the front door.

Rachel held her breath and gnawed on a fingernail as Bishop Wagler moved to the front door, grasped the handle, and jerked it open. As though the frog knew who was in charge, it jumped right out the door. Jacob and Martin put the bench back in place. Everyone sat down, and the singing started again as if nothing unusual had happened.

When church ended, the men and boys put their black felt hats on their heads and filed out of the house. Next, the younger girls left. The women and older girls went to the kitchen to prepare the meal. Rachel started for the door, but Mom grasped her hand. "Do you know anything about that frog?" she asked, staring hard at Rachel.

Rachel nodded. She bit her lips so she wouldn't smile. Now that it was over, she realized it had been funny to see the frog land in Sarah King's and Elsie Byler's laps and down Aaron King's shirt. But she was sure her mother didn't share those feelings.

"Sorry, Mom," Rachel said. "I wanted to have a frog race this afternoon, and I didn't think the frogs would get out of the box."

"Frogs?" Mom repeated.

Ribbet! Ribbet!

Mom turned to look at the box sitting on the utility porch. "How many more frogs did you bring, Rachel?"

"Just one." Rachel hurried to the box and picked it up. "I'll take this outside right away."

Mom nodded. "We'll talk about this little escapade when we get home." As Mom turned and walked away, Rachel heard her mutter, "Always trouble somewhere!"

Rachel tried to think of some way to get out of punishment, but she figured nothing would help her this time. She had been lucky to get off without a *bletsching* this morning after she'd ruined the eggs. And she was certainly fortunate that the frogs had apparently made her mother forget about Bishop Wagler hearing her ugly words.

"You brought the frogs, didn't you?" Mary asked when Rachel stepped outside. Rachel nodded. "I thought it would be fun to have a race with them after church."

"Are you in big trouble? Do you think you'll get a spanking?" Mary asked.

"Maybe. Or I might have extra chores to do." Rachel set the box on the ground, lifted the lid, and watched frog number two hop away.

Mary flopped onto the grass under a willow tree. Rachel dropped beside her. "It would be nice to have church out here where it's cooler, don't you think?" her cousin asked.

"Jah, and those benches can get pretty hard after a while," Rachel agreed.

"I know, but we couldn't have church outside during the winter."

Rachel snatched a blade of grass and bit off the end. At least it was better than chewing her nails. "You'll never guess what I got Friday night," she said, thinking a different subject would make her feel better.

"What?"

"Guess."

"Did your mamm make you a new dress?"

Rachel shook her head. "She probably won't do that until right before school starts again."

Mary's pale eyebrows wiggled together, and she rubbed her chin. "Hmm. . . Did you get some licorice? I know that's your favorite candy."

"That's not it, either. *Gebscht uff?*"

Her cousin nodded. "Jah, I give up. What did you get?"

"A bussli."

"That's great. Now our two cats can play

together," Mary said excitedly. "Where did you get the kitten? What's its name?"

Rachel explained about being trapped in the Millers' root cellar and how Missy and her kittens had kept her company. She told Mary that Rudy had brought Cuddles over as a surprise gift from Howard Miller.

"You must have been scared down there in that cellar," Mary said, her eyes opening wide.

Rachel was about to tell her how horrible it had been, but the girls were called to join the women for their noon meal.

Rachel sat between her mother and sister at a long picnic table. Mary sat across from Rachel, between her own mother and sister. The meal included hot bean soup, ham-and-cheese sandwiches, and lots of cold milk to drink. For dessert, Anna Miller served apple and cherry pie. Rachel ate until she couldn't take another bite. Then she patted her stomach and looked at the clear, blue sky. The sun felt warm against her face, and for the moment she forgot about the mean goose, broken eggs, and hopping frogs that had nearly ruined her day. She sighed as clouds covered the warm sun. As hard as she tried to steer clear of trouble, trouble always seemed to find her.

Just then, a drop of water splattered on Rachel's

nose. It was followed by another and another. "Oh, no, it's starting to rain!" she moaned.

What was the use of school being out if it was going to rain all summer? Rachel sighed. Even the weather was causing trouble in her life!

Chapter 5

Where Is Summer?

Flinging the back door open wide, Rachel rushed into the kitchen. "It's raining again! Can you believe it, Mom? How many more days of rain are we gonna have?" She stood inside the door, dripping wet and frowning. Ever since the frog episode during church, she'd had extra chores to do, and doing them in the rain wasn't much fun.

Mom was cutting quilting material at the kitchen table, but she looked at Rachel and smiled. "Rain is good for the garden, and the crops in the fields need it, as well."

"But, Mom, where is summer? All we've had for a couple of weeks now is rain, rain, rain."

"Sunshine will come again soon," her mother answered. "Now, you're dripping water all over my clean floor, and if you don't get out of that wet dress soon, you'll likely catch a cold."

Rachel shrugged and headed for the stairs. What was the use in complaining to Mom? No one in her family seemed to understand how she felt about anything. Rachel wondered if her mother ever remembered what it was like to be young.

When Rachel entered her room, she found Cuddles lying at the foot of her bed. She hurried across the room and shook her finger in the kitten's face. "You know what Mom would say if she caught you napping on my bed. She doesn't want you in the house, much less up on the furniture. And you'd get me in big trouble."

Rachel stroked the kitten's soft, silky head. "Guess I can't really blame you for sneaking in. The weather's too awful to be doing anything but sleeping on a soft, warm bed."

Cuddles responded with a lazy stretch and a faint *meow*. Then she began to purr.

Rachel slipped out of her wet clothes and into a clean dress and hurried to the window. Pressing her nose against the glass, she groaned. "Sure wish I could be at the creek today instead of cooped up in this stuffy old house. It's supposed to be summer, and I'm bored. There must be something fun I can do."

The kitten's loud purr turned to a soft rumble, but she didn't open her eyes.

A knock sounded on Rachel's bedroom door, and she called out, "Come in!"

The door squeaked open, and Jacob poked his head inside. "Mom went out to the barn to check on the calf that was born yesterday. She wants you to help Esther start supper." When he spotted Cuddles on Rachel's bed, he shook his head and said, "You'd better put that cat outside. You know Mom doesn't like—"

"I know, I know," Rachel interrupted. "But it's raining, and it's not fair to make my sweet little bussli stay outdoors in this awful weather." She sat on the bed beside Cuddles, just in case her brother decided to haul the kitten outside.

"Aw, you're silly. Animals don't mind the rain," Jacob said with a grunt.

"They do so," Rachel argued. "The cows always head straight for the barn whenever it rains. Even the chickens have the good sense to stay in their coop until the sun comes out."

Jacob waved his hand like he was shooing away a pesky fly. "Well, if Mom catches that cat on your bed, you'll be in big trouble."

"You're not going to tell, are you?" Rachel figured she had enough problems with the extra chores she'd been assigned.

"Naw, but you'd better hurry and get downstairs before Mom comes back inside and wonders why you're not helping Esther."

"*Danki*, Jacob."

"You're welcome."

Rachel was a bit surprised that Jacob was being so nice. It seemed like he usually liked to see her get in trouble. She stroked Cuddles's paw and headed downstairs to help her sister.

The rain continued all that week, and Rachel complained about it almost every day. "If summer doesn't get here soon, it'll be over. Then school will start again, and I won't have had any fun at all," she announced during supper one evening.

"Summer will come. It always does," Pap said from his place at the head of the table. "The rain's put us behind in our fieldwork, but we should still be glad for it. It could be the only rain we'll have all summer."

"I hope it is. This awful weather has kept me from playing outdoors." Rachel pointed to the container sitting near Esther. "Pass the pickles, please."

"If you want something fun to do, maybe you should put on your thinking cap and come up with something you will enjoy." Esther pointed to Rachel's plate. "And you already have two pickles."

Rachel frowned. She didn't even remember taking the pickles. Maybe that was because she was so upset over the rain.

"If you're bored, you can come to the barn and help me brush the horses," said Henry. "I think that's fun, and you're always pestering me to let you help."

"*Humph!* You always tell me that brushing horses is men's work." Rachel bit into one of her pickles and puckered her lips. She liked the tangy flavor of garlic and dill, but it made the edges of her mouth pull together.

"It *is* men's work," Henry answered with a wink. "But just this once, I might let you help."

Rachel shrugged her shoulders. "I'll think about it."

"Maybe you'd like to help me do some quilting. I find that to be enjoyable," Mom said, forking another piece of ham onto her plate.

Rachel shook her head. "I'd probably end up pricking my finger with the needle, like I usually do whenever I try to sew."

"I've got an idea," Esther said. "Why don't the two of us do some baking? We can make one of your favorites—banana chocolate chip cookies."

Rachel pushed her chair away from the table

and began to clear her dishes. "I'm not really in the mood for baking, either."

"Well, young lady, it seems as if all you want to do is grumble and complain. So after you wash the dishes, I think it might be a good idea if you head on up to bed," Pap said firmly. "Maybe if you sleep off this bad mood, you'll wake up happier in the morning."

"Jah, you go around looking like you've been sucking on a slice of dill pickle," Jacob put in.

Rachel thought about the verse of scripture from Proverbs 17:22 that Pap had read to them one evening before bed. It said: "A cheerful heart is good medicine, but a crushed spirit dries up the bones." She knew the Bible verse didn't actually mean her bones would dry up if she wasn't happy, but she got the point, just the same.

"I'll help Esther make cookies," she said as she ran water into the kitchen sink.

"And no more complaining?" Pap asked.

She shook her head.

"*Der Herr sie gedankt*," Mom whispered. "Jah, thank the Lord."

When Rachel finished the dishes, she helped her sister set out the items they would need for the cookies.

"Why don't you mix the dry ingredients?"

Esther suggested. "I'll beat the eggs and mix all of the wet ingredients."

Rachel frowned. "How come you get to do the fun part? Why can't I beat the eggs?"

Esther handed Rachel a large bowl and the eggbeater. "You can mix whatever part of the cookie batter you want."

Rachel thanked her sister and went to the refrigerator to get out two eggs. When she cracked the first one into the bowl, a piece of eggshell fell in, as well. "Who said making cookies was fun?" she grumbled as she stuck her fingers into the gooey egg whites and pulled out the shell.

"You said you wanted to beat the eggs," Esther reminded. "Would you rather I do that part while you mix the dry ingredients?"

Rachel nodded and slid over to the other side of the counter, where Esther had already placed a sack of flour and a can of shortening.

"Don't forget the baking powder and salt," her sister said. "They're still in the cupboard."

Rachel slid a wooden stool to the cupboard and climbed up. "Whoa!" She almost lost her balance but kept herself from falling by grabbing the handle on the cupboard door.

"Are you okay?" Esther asked. "Would you like me to do that for you?"

"I'm fine." Rachel reached into the cupboard for the box of salt and leaned down to set it on the counter. *Let's see now. Does the recipe call for baking powder or soda?* She squinted at the spice containers and boxes of other baking ingredients. *I probably should ask Esther, but then she might think I'm* dumm *and don't know anything.*

Rachel grabbed the box of baking soda and placed it beside the salt. Then she reached for a package of white sugar and climbed down.

When the ingredients were all mixed and the cookies were put in the oven, Rachel could hardly wait to get a bite. They smelled so good! Finally it was time to grab a pot holder and take the first batch of cookies out of the oven. Rachel waited until they had cooled before she ate one. "Something is wrong with these cookies," she said, wrinkling her nose. "Maybe the banana you put in wasn't ripe enough, Esther."

"I'm sure it was." Esther lifted a cookie from the cooling rack and took a bite. "Eww. . .these do taste funny. How much sugar did you put in, Rachel?"

"Half a cup, I think."

Esther shook her head. "You were supposed to use one full cup, so that's why the cookies aren't sweet enough."

"Oh. Guess I got *verhuddelt*. It seems I get confused a lot lately."

"The cookies aren't puffed up the way they should be, either. How much baking powder did you use?" her sister asked.

"I. . .uh. . .thought I was supposed to use baking *soda*."

"The ingredients for the cookies are right there on top of Mom's recipe file," Esther said, pointing to the small metal box on the cupboard. "It seems that you didn't follow the directions for the dry ingredients."

"Trouble again," Rachel mumbled. "Maybe I should have helped Henry with the horses instead of trying to make cookies." She hung her head. "I guess I'm nothing but trouble. I can't seem to do anything right these days."

"You just need to pay more attention to what you're doing," Esther said, giving Rachel a hug. "We can add more sugar and some baking powder to the rest of the cookie dough. Would you like to mix them in?"

Rachel shook her head. "No, thanks. I think I'll go to my room and get ready for bed." Rachel ran out of the kitchen and dashed up the stairs.

When Rachel entered her room, she flopped onto the bed. As she lay there feeling sorry for herself, she studied the cracks in the ceiling. They reminded her of a jigsaw puzzle. She hoped Mom wouldn't find out about the cookies. She didn't want to get into trouble for wasting food.

Boom! A crash of thunder reminded her of the whole reason she'd been inside messing up cookies anyway.

"I hope summer will hurry up and get here," she muttered. "It will be my birthday soon, and it won't be any fun if we have to eat supper in the house that night." Mom had told Rachel that they might have a picnic in the backyard for her birthday.

Rachel licked her lips as she thought about juicy, plump hot dogs roasting over the coals of Pap's barbecue pit. She could almost taste Mom's tangy potato salad and smell the spicy pickled beets.

"Sure hope I get some fun gifts this year," she murmured. She hoped for a skateboard and had even dropped a few hints to her family.

Suddenly, an idea popped into Rachel's mind, and she sprang to her feet. "If I had enough money, I could buy my own skateboard. I probably won't get one for my birthday anyway. It seems like I always get gifts that are practical instead of fun."

Rachel rushed to her dresser and jerked open the top drawer. She pulled out a small, blue bank shaped like a pig and held it over her bed, shaking the contents until all the money fell onto her patchwork quilt. She counted out six dollars and fifty cents. The skateboard she had seen at Kauffman's Store cost fifteen dollars, so she would need another eight and a half dollars to buy it.

Rachel tapped her finger against her chin. "I wonder how I can earn the rest of the money before my birthday gets here. Maybe I could sell something to Noah Kauffman. Lots of tourists look in his store for Amish-made items, so I might be able to make something they would like."

Rachel dropped the coins back into the bank. "I'm sure I can come up with a few things to sell before our next trip to town." She flopped onto the bed and stroked Cuddles, who had found her way into Rachel's room once again. "With a skateboard, I could sail up and down the sidewalks in town, the way I've seen so many other kinner do. Maybe I could even ride it to and from school every day. Then I would get there quicker, and I'd be home earlier, too." She patted the top of her kitten's silky head. "And it would give me more time to spend with you, my furry little friend."

Cuddles licked the end of Rachel's finger with her small, pink tongue.

"A skateboard wouldn't be nearly as exciting as

riding in a car, but it would be faster than walking." Rachel pressed her face close to the kitten's nose. "I still want to go for a ride in a fancy, fast car someday, but until then, a skateboard will have to do."

Cuddles gave Rachel another sandpapery kiss, this time on her nose.

"Maybe you'd like to go for a ride on my new skateboard. Would you like that, Cuddles? Would you, girl?"

The kitten was falling asleep, for her eyes had closed, and her only response now was a soft, gentle purr. Rachel felt sleepy, too. She nestled against her pillow, dreaming about soaring with Cuddles on a shiny new skateboard.

Chapter 6

Fireflies and Secrets

By the end of June, the rain finally stopped. Sunshine and warmer weather took over, so Rachel could spend more time outdoors. She played with Cuddles, climbed her favorite tree, and waded in the creek. She plodded back and forth in the cool water now, trying not to get the edge of her long, blue dress wet.

As Rachel stepped carefully across some slippery rocks, she thought about her kitten and how much she loved her. She thought about the tasty apple pie she'd had for breakfast that morning. And she thought about her birthday and wondered what gifts she might get. Two weeks earlier, she and Esther had gone to town to buy groceries. She had taken some of the pet rocks she'd painted to Kauffman's Store. Noah Kauffman

had said they were nice. He especially liked the
ones she had made to look like ladybugs. He'd
taken the rocks on consignment, which meant if he
sold any, Rachel would get half of the money and
he would get the other half. She hoped that by the
time they went to town again all the rocks would
have been sold. Then she could buy the green and
silver skateboard she had put on layaway with her
piggy bank money.

"Rachel! Come up to the house, *schnell*," Mom
called.

Rachel shielded her eyes from the glare of the
sun and squinted. She saw Mom standing on the
back porch, with her hands cupped around her
mouth, and wondered why she wanted her to come
quickly.

"Rachel! Schnell!"

"I'm coming, Mom." Rachel plodded out of the
creek, remembering the last time she hadn't come
when Mom had called. No way was she doing
laundry again!

Up in the yard, Rachel found Pap lighting the
barbecue, while Henry and Jacob moved the picnic
table under the shade of a maple tree. "Are we
having a picnic?" she asked her oldest brother.

Henry nodded. "Mom and Esther are in the
kitchen getting everything ready, so you'd better

hurry inside to help."

Rachel bounded up the stairs. She loved picnics!

A short time later, the Yoders gathered around the picnic table. After their silent prayer, Mom passed the food. They had grilled hot dogs, tangy potato salad, spicy pickled beets, maple-flavored baked beans, and plenty of Pap's icy-cold, homemade root beer.

Rachel had second helpings of everything. By the time she'd finished eating, she could hardly breathe. "Yum. Everything tasted wunderbaar," she said, licking her fingers.

"You do have a napkin," Mom said, shaking her head.

Rachel glanced at the wadded napkin in her lap. It was a lot more fun to lick your fingers than to wipe them on a plain old napkin. Still, she didn't want to risk getting in trouble with Mom, so she blotted her lips on one corner of the napkin and said, "May I please have the empty beet jar?"

Mom gave Rachel a curious look over the top of her glasses. "Whatever for?"

"I want to catch fireflies."

Her mother shrugged and handed Rachel the jar. "You'd better rinse it out well, or those poor little bugs might turn purple."

"I will, Mom." Rachel ran into the house to

rinse the jar in the sink. A short time later, she returned with the clean jar in one hand and her kitten tucked under her arm. "Cuddles and I are going to take a nap," she said as she passed Esther, who sat on the porch swing, reading a book. "We got up extra early this morning. Could you wake me when the fireflies start to shine?"

"I would, but Rudy's coming to take me for a drive. He wants to see how well his new horse pulls the buggy."

"I'll ask someone else then." Rachel had only taken a few steps when Esther called out to her.

"You're not going to kill those poor fireflies, are you?"

Rachel shook her head. " 'Course not. I just want to give myself some light when I go to bed tonight."

"Ah, I see." Esther left the swing and joined Rachel on the step. "Are you afraid of the dark?"

"Maybe. . ." Rachel really didn't want to answer Esther's question.

"Why don't you use a flashlight?"

"The batteries went dead the last time I tried that."

Esther shrugged. "I hope the fireflies work out for you then."

Cuddles meowed as Rachel headed across the

yard. She leaned down and kissed the kitten on the nose. She noticed Mom and Pap walking by the garden, and decided it would be best not to bother them. Then she passed by the picnic table and spotted Jacob and Henry playing a game of checkers. She stopped and tapped Jacob on the shoulder.

"What do you want, Rachel?" he asked, as he took two of Henry's checkers.

"Cuddles and I are gonna rest awhile. Will you wake me when the fireflies start to rise and shine?"

"Jah, sure," Jacob mumbled.

"Danki." Rachel wandered to the tallest maple tree in their yard and sat on the grass. She set the empty jar down, placed Cuddles across her chest, and leaned against the tree trunk. She felt so tired, and Cuddles's gentle purring soon put her to sleep.

Whoo-hoo! Whoo-hoo! Whoo-hoo! Rachel's eyes popped open. She could barely see the great horned owl that looked down at her from a branch in the tree. She sat up quickly and glanced around the yard, wondering how long she had been asleep. It was almost dark, and Rachel could see the fireflies as they fluttered up from the grass.

"Why didn't somebody wake me?" She set Cuddles on the ground, reached for the glass jar, and scrambled to her feet.

Rachel was about to chase the fireflies, when she heard voices. She noticed that Henry and Jacob were still at the picnic table. They weren't playing checkers, but their heads were close together.

"This needs to be kept secret," Henry said quietly. Rachel stopped and listened closely, but she could barely hear him. "We can't tell anyone, okay?"

Jacob nodded. "I won't say a word. I promise."

Secrets? Promises? What was going on? Rachel hurried to the picnic table and nudged Jacob's arm. "What were you and Henry talking about?"

Jacob looked at his older brother, and Henry shook his head. Then Jacob looked back at Rachel and said, "We weren't talkin' about much at all."

"But you said something about a secret," she persisted. "What kind of secret are you keeping?"

Henry tweaked the end of Rachel's nose. "You'll find out soon enough, snoopy sister."

"I'm not snoopy. I just—"

"Say, why aren't you out there catching lightning bugs?" Jacob asked, changing the subject. "I thought that's why you wanted the empty jar."

Rachel pointed to her brother and frowned. "Because someone forgot to wake me, and they're *fireflies* not *lightning bugs*."

"Jah, well, I've heard 'em called *lightning bugs,*" Jacob said. "Only a bensel would call them *fireflies.*"

Henry snickered. "I guess they get the name *lightning bug* because the light on their stomach flashes off and on."

"That's right. Put several of those critters inside a jar, and you'll have enough light to read by." Jacob poked Rachel's arm. "Since you're awake now, don't you think you'd better get busy and capture those *lightning bugs* before it's time to go to bed?"

"Well, if you won't tell me your secret, I guess I will try to see how many *fireflies* I can catch." No way would Rachel call them *lightning bugs* just because Jacob said that's what they were. She hurried away, and when she came to a spot in the grass where several fireflies had risen, she dropped to her knees. A few minutes later, Rachel had the jar filled with dancing, glowing bugs.

Lights on. Lights off. Lights on. The insects' shimmering stomachs twinkled and lit up the whole jar.

"This is perfect. Now when Mom tells me to put out the oil lamp by my bed, I can still read." Rachel smiled.

Inside the house, Rachel found Mom and Pap playing Scrabble. "I was about to call you," Mom said, nodding at Rachel. "It's time for you to get ready for bed."

Rachel didn't argue. Since she had her jar of lights, this was one time she didn't mind going to bed. She hugged Mom and Pap and gave each a kiss on the cheek. Then she said good night and scampered up the stairs.

Rachel set the jar of fireflies on the small table by her bed and opened the window. She was glad there was a tall maple tree growing outside her window. That gave Cuddles a way to get inside. Then she undressed and slipped into her long, cotton nightgown. Next she headed for the bathroom to wash her face and brush her teeth.

A few minutes later, Rachel returned to her room and knelt by her bed to say her prayers. "Heavenly Father, bless everyone in my family, and let the angels surround my bed as I sleep through the night. Amen."

She picked up her favorite book, turned down the oil lamp, shut the window, and crawled into bed next to an already-sleeping Cuddles.

Rachel held the book close to the jar, but to her surprise, no light came from it. She tapped on the side of the glass. Still nothing. No twinkling lights. Not a single one.

"What's going on?" Rachel set the book aside

and grasped the lid on the jar. She twisted the lid off and peered inside. "Hmm. . .maybe they've fallen asleep." She jiggled the jar this way and that. "Wake up you sleepy fireflies, and give me some light."

Suddenly, the room began to glow, as tiny, shimmering fireflies flittered toward the ceiling. Some flew to the left. Some soared to the right. Some drifted down and landed on Rachel's stomach.

"I'm all lit up!" She jumped out of bed, and some of the fireflies went with her. Reaching out with one hand, and then quickly with the other, she ran around the room, chasing the fireflies and laughing so hard her sides ached.

Cuddles woke up and joined the chase, leaping into the air and swatting at the fireflies with her paws.

"What's all the ruckus about?" Mom said as she burst into Rachel's room. She stopped just inside the door. "Oh, Rachel, what have you done?"

"The fireflies quit glowing, so I opened the jar lid, and then—"

"We've got to get them out of here," Mom said as she clapped her hands together.

"Please, don't hurt any of them," Rachel pleaded. "I'll try to get every bug back into the jar."

"And how do you plan to get them back in that jar?"

Rachel thought a minute. Mom was probably right. It would be hard to capture all those bugs. An idea popped into Rachel's head. She rushed across the room, pulled up the window shade, and opened the window as wide as it would go. The cool evening breeze blew in, lifting Rachel's long hair so it fell against her face. A few seconds later, little bugs blinking off and on sailed out her window and into the night sky.

Rachel lit the oil lamp and looked around the room. "I think they're all gone."

"So it would seem." Mom moved past Rachel and shut the window. "Now into bed with you. From now on, there will be no more critters in this room." She bent over and picked up Rachel's cat, who sat in front of the window, meowing for all she was worth. "And that includes busslin with *fleh!*"

"I'm sure Cuddles doesn't have fleas, and she likes it here with me."

Mom shook her head. "The kitten belongs in the barn, not in your room."

"If Cuddles had a flea collar, then could she come inside?"

Mom tapped her chin as she tipped her head. "We'll see." She left the bedroom, carrying

Cuddles and muttering, "Immer druwwle eiyets."

Rachel crawled back into bed with a grunt. Such a day this had turned out to be. There were secrets no one wanted her to know, bugs that wouldn't shine when they should, and now Cuddles had been taken back to the barn, with no promise of ever being allowed in Rachel's room.

Rachel felt lonely without her kitten and a bit nervous because the room was so dark again. To help her feel less afraid, she sang one of her favorite church songs, "*Das Lob Lied*," which was "The Hymn of Praise." It reminded her to praise God, even when things weren't going the way she wanted them to.

"Have a good night, Lord," she whispered as her eyes drifted shut. "I'll talk to You in the morning. And please help me stay out of trouble."

Chapter 7

Birthday Surprises

On the day before Rachel's birthday, she and Esther went to town so Esther could get some fabric she needed for her wedding dress. Rachel asked to go to Kauffman's to see if any of her painted rocks had sold.

"Sure," Esther agreed. "After we finish our errands, I'll take you out for a late breakfast." She tapped Rachel on the shoulder. "In the meantime, I'm going to the quilt shop across the street to look at some material. I'll be back for you in half an hour."

"Okay." Rachel hurried into the store, full of excitement. *If all my rocks have sold, I might be able to take my new skateboard home today,* Rachel thought as she headed to the display case to see the green and silver skateboard that would soon be hers. She skidded to a stop. The skateboard was gone. The case only displayed a pair of roller skates, a baseball glove, and a few jump ropes. *He's sold it! Noah Kauffman sold my skateboard.* Tears filled Rachel's eyes, and she bit her bottom lip, struggling not to cry.

When Noah finished waiting on a customer, he walked up to Rachel and said, "Good morning, Rachel. Have you come to collect your money for the painted rocks I've sold?"

She sighed. Money? What good was money if she couldn't have the skateboard?

"All your rocks are gone, and I have your consignment money waiting," he said with a smile.

"But the skateboard I wanted to buy is gone."

Noah nodded. "The one you put on layaway, right?"

"You said you'd keep it until I had enough money, but it's not there anymore."

"It's still in the store. I keep my layaways in the back room," Mr. Kauffman said.

"Am I ever glad to hear that!" Rachel exclaimed. "Should we take care of the money matter now?"

"Jah, please."

"Your part of the profit is five dollars."

Rachel's smile quickly turned to a frown. "Is that all?"

Noah nodded. "I charged one dollar for each of your rocks, and your half for ten rocks is five dollars."

"But that's not nearly enough for the skateboard."

"Do you have any more painted rocks to sell?" he asked. "The tourists seem to like them. Especially the ones you painted to look like ladybugs and turtles."

Rachel shook her head. "I would need to paint more, and since my birthday is tomorrow, I had hoped to get the skateboard today."

"I'm sorry, Rachel," Noah said. "I guess it will have to be a late birthday present."

With her head down and her shoulders slumped, Rachel walked away. She would wait for Esther outside. If she stayed in the store, she would only think about the wonderful, shiny skateboard she wouldn't be riding on her birthday.

As Rachel waited on the sidewalk, she stood with her arms folded, watching plain horse and buggies and shiny, fast cars pass on the street. When she spotted an English boy riding a skateboard on the sidewalk, she felt worse.

It's not fair that I can't have my new skateboard today, she thought. *If I can't find the time to paint any more rocks, I may never have enough money to get the skateboard off layaway.*

Rachel closed her eyes and tried to think about something else—anything to get her mind off the skateboard she wouldn't have in time for her birthday.

When Rachel heard someone clear their throat, she opened her eyes. It was Esther coming to take her to breakfast. At least that was something to smile about.

A short time later, Rachel and Esther sat in a booth at the restaurant. "What would you like to order?" their waitress asked, looking at Esther.

Esther smiled at the young English woman. "I think I'll have a blueberry waffle and a cup of hot tea." She glanced over at Rachel. "Would you like to place your own order, or would you rather I do it for you?"

"I can do it." Rachel looked up at the waitress and said, "I'd like my waffle to be strawberry, please. Oh, and I would also like to have a glass of grape fruit juice."

The waitress raised her dark eyebrows and flipped her ponytail with one hand. "Are you sure that's the kind of juice you want?"

Rachel nodded. Of course she was sure. She wouldn't have ordered it if she wasn't sure.

The waitress shrugged, wrote Rachel's order on her tablet, and walked away.

While they waited for their meal, Rachel asked Esther, "Did you get the material you wanted for your wedding dress?"

Esther smiled. "I found just the right shade of blue. I also bought the white material I'll need to make the apron." She nodded at Rachel. "How about you? Did you buy anything at Kauffman's Store?"

Rachel shook her head. "Not really." She was tempted to tell her sister about the skateboard she had put on layaway but decided it would be best not to mention it right now. Esther might think Rachel was selfish for wanting to buy her own birthday present. Besides, she didn't have the skateboard and might never own it if she couldn't earn enough money. "I'm sure glad we haven't had any more rain lately," she said, changing the subject.

Esther glanced out the window. "This day has started off warm, so a nice rain shower would be very gut."

Rachel was about to argue the point when their waitress arrived with Esther's tea and a glass of strange-looking juice for Rachel. Instead of purple, like grape juice should be, it was yellow.

Rachel reached for the glass and sipped. "Ugh! This isn't sweet like grape fruit juice."

"It's what you ordered," the waitress said.

Rachel shook her head. "No, I—"

"You said you wanted a glass of grapefruit juice, and that's what I brought you. I'll be right back with your breakfast." The waitress walked away before Rachel could say anything more.

Rachel frowned and puckered her lips.

"What's wrong?" Esther asked, leaning toward Rachel. "Don't you like grapefruit juice?"

"I—I thought I had ordered grape juice, not this sour-tasting stuff." She lifted her glass and wrinkled her nose. "Do I have to drink this?"

"What do you think Mom or Pap would say about that?"

"They'd probably say it would be wasteful not to drink it."

Esther reached across the table and picked up Rachel's glass. "Then I shall drink it for you, and you can order the right kind of juice this time."

Rachel breathed a sigh of relief. "Danki, Esther." She hated to cause trouble, but she was sure glad she didn't have to drink it!

Her sister smiled. "You are most welcome."

Rachel awoke the next morning, knowing that today was her tenth birthday and that the one thing she wanted most still sat in the back of

Kauffman's Store. Maybe after she finished her chores for the day, she could paint more rocks for consignment. However, she still wouldn't get the skateboard today.

When Rachel entered the kitchen, she found her mother standing near the cupboard.

"*Guder mariye*. Happy birthday," said Mom.

"Good morning. Where is everyone?" Rachel asked.

"Pap, Henry, and Jacob are outside doing their chores. Esther went somewhere with Rudy, and they'll eat breakfast out." Mom nodded toward the cupboard across the room. "Would you please get out the maple syrup? I've fixed some buttermilk pancakes this morning, and they're keeping warm in the oven."

Rachel went to the cupboard and took the syrup down from the shelf.

"If you will please set the table, we can eat as soon as the men come inside," Mom said as she took some butter from the refrigerator.

Rachel hurried to get the dishes and silverware out. She had just placed the glasses on the table when the back door creaked open. Henry and Jacob clomped into the kitchen.

"Pap will be right in," Henry told Mom as he went to the sink to wash his hands. When he finished, he turned to Rachel and said, "Happy birthday, sister."

Rachel noticed that Jacob held his arms behind his back, like he might be hiding something. She craned her neck to see what it was, but he kept turning this way and that to block her view. "Can I open my gifts before we eat?" Rachel asked.

"Gifts? Who said anything about gifts?" Pap said as he stepped into the kitchen.

Rachel giggled. "I think you're teasing me. Jacob and Henry must have a gift because they look guilty, and Jacob's hiding something behind his back."

Pap chuckled, causing his beard to jiggle up and down. "So, who wants to go first?"

"We will." Jacob held his hands in front of him, revealing a homemade wooden skateboard with shiny chrome wheels. "Henry and I have been working on this for weeks."

Rachel's mouth dropped open. "Is—is this the secret you were whispering about the other night?"

Henry nodded, and Jacob grinned.

"I—I hardly know what to say," she stammered.

"We knew you wanted a skateboard," Jacob said, handing it to her.

"Jah, you've dropped plenty of hints," Henry put in.

"I know, but I didn't think I would ever get one, so I—" Rachel's voice trailed off. How could she tell her brothers that she had put her own skateboard on layaway? The homemade skateboard wasn't nearly as beautiful as the green and silver one at Kauffman's Store, but she knew it would hurt her brothers' feelings if she refused their gift. So Rachel took the skateboard and smiled. "Danki, Jacob. Danki, Henry."

"You're welcome," they both said.

Rachel wondered what she would do with two skateboards if she went ahead and bought the skateboard at Kauffman's. Should she tell Noah to take the fancy one off layaway and then spend her money on something else? *I'll figure that out later,* she decided. *Right now I just want to enjoy my birthday.*

"Now it's my turn," Mom said as she headed across the room to her sewing cabinet. She removed a small basket and handed it to Rachel.

Rachel set the skateboard on the floor and opened the lid of the basket. Inside were some pins, needles, thread, scissors, and several small pieces of material.

"I thought it was time you had your own sewing basket," Mom said.

Rachel didn't like to sew. She would much rather be outside playing with Cuddles, climbing a tree, or wading in the creek. But she didn't want to hurt her mother's feelings, so she smiled and said, "Danki, Mom."

Mom smiled and nodded, then she nudged Pap's arm with her elbow. "It's your turn, Levi."

Pap opened the front of his shirt and pulled out a small package wrapped in brown paper. He handed it to Rachel and winked. "This is just for fun."

Rachel opened Pap's present. Inside, she found a bag of licorice and a large metal ring with a handle on one end. "Licorice is my favorite candy," she said with a grin.

Pap nodded. "Jah, I know. It's my favorite, too."

Rachel picked up the metal ring. "What's this, Pap?"

"It's a bubble blower. You just need a bowl full of soapy water with a squirt of glycerin added. Then you'll be all set. With this special ring, you can make bigger bubbles than you ever imagined."

Rachel gave her father a hug. "I guess I will."

"You've received some nice birthday gifts," Mom said, "but I think we should eat now." She opened the oven and removed the baking dish filled with pancakes, and everyone gathered around the table.

"Let's pray, and then we'll eat," Pap said with a nod.

Rachel enjoyed every bite of the delicious buttermilk pancakes Mom had made. When they finished their meal and Rachel had helped clean the kitchen, she decided to try out the bubble maker Pap had made for her.

She stepped onto the back porch and sat on the top step. She set the pan of soapy water Mom had fixed next to her and dipped the metal wand into it. When she pulled the wand out and waved it in the breeze, she was surprised to see a huge bubble. It blew lazily across the yard. Rachel laughed, then quickly made more bubbles. Cuddles, who had been lying beside Rachel, sprang to her feet and jumped off the porch. The kitten dashed into the yard after the colorful bubbles, but just as her paw touched a bubble, it popped and disappeared.

"You *kischblich* bussli! Here are some more bubbles for you to chase." Rachel waved the wand again and again, laughing each time Cuddles thought she could catch the shiny, see-through balls.

"It looks as though you're having fun. Mind if I join you?"

Rachel turned and looked up at Pap, who stood behind her. She had been so busy playing that she hadn't heard him come out the door. "You want to blow some bubbles?" she asked.

"If you don't mind sharing the wand." Pap sat on the step beside her.

"Of course I don't mind." Rachel handed the metal ring to her father, and he dipped it into the soapy water. Instead of waving the wand as she had done, he blew gently on it. A fat bubble formed. As it started to leave the ring, Pap blew again, causing a second bubble to form and stick to the first one. He blew one more time, and a third bubble stuck to the first two. Then he waved the ring slightly, and the three bubbles, still held together, sailed across the yard.

Rachel clapped her hands. "Oh, Pap, you've made a triple! I've made doubles with my plastic bubble blower before, but I've never made a triple!"

"Look at all the different colors—pink, purple, blue, yellow, and green." Pap seemed almost as excited as Rachel. The twinkle in his clear blue eyes let her know he was having a good time.

"The colorful bubbles remind me of a rainbow," she said.

He nodded. "That's right, and the rainbow reminds me that the world God made is full of beauty."

"Like all the pretty flowers in Mom's garden," Rachel said dreamily. "Each one is full of beautiful colors."

Rachel noticed a faraway look in Pap's eyes as he stared across the yard. "I've enjoyed looking at flowers ever since I was a boy. My older brothers often teased me about it, though," he said with a wink.

Rachel reached over and grabbed her father's hand, squeezing it. So far her birthday had gone better than she'd expected.

Chapter 8

Skateboard Troubles

Rachel was eager to try out her new skateboard, so after Pap and her brothers headed to the fields to work, she put her new bubble wand in her room and took the skateboard outside. Mom had forbidden Rachel to ride on the paved road in front of their farm, saying it was too dangerous. So Rachel knew she would have to find another place to try it out. The graveled driveway was out of the question because the wheels would never roll smoothly over the rocks. The grass had too many bumps, so that wouldn't do. The wooden floor in the barn might work, though.

Holding the skateboard under one arm and calling Cuddles to follow, Rachel headed for the barn.

As soon as she stepped through the door, she

realized that the barn was definitely big enough for skateboarding. Unfortunately, most of the floor was covered with bales of hay piled on it.

Rachel groaned and flopped onto one of the bales to think. Maybe she could move the hay out of the way to create a path for skateboarding. However, that seemed like a lot of trouble, and she probably couldn't move the heavy bales alone. "There must be somewhere I can try out the skateboard Henry and Jacob worked so hard to make for my birthday."

Finally an idea popped into her head. She jumped up, grabbed the skateboard, and dashed out of the barn. She looked around the yard and spotted Mom hanging laundry on the clothesline. If she hurried, she thought she could make it to the house without being seen.

Rachel scampered to the back door, slipped inside, and scurried up the stairs with Cuddles on her heels. She screeched to a stop in the hallway and studied the long wooden floor. It had been freshly polished and looked like the perfect place to try her skateboard. Cuddles stopped, too, only she curled up in a corner and quickly fell asleep.

Rachel stood at one end of the hall and placed the skateboard on the floor. She had watched other children in town ride their skateboards up and down the sidewalks, so she knew how to stand. Put one foot on the board, the other one on the ground, and push off. It looked easy enough.

Rachel soon discovered that keeping her balance was the hardest part. It wasn't easy to hold her body upright and move forward at the same time. Soon after she had pushed off, the skateboard sailed down the hallway, and she swayed back and forth like a tree branch in the wind. "This is so much fun!"

In spite of the trouble Rachel had remaining upright, she enjoyed the ride, although it didn't seem nearly long enough. By the time she had made four trips up and back, she was able to keep her balance fairly well.

"Look at me, Cuddles," she called to her sleeping cat. "I'm having such a good time!"

Cuddles opened one eye and replied with a *meow*. Then she curled her paws under her head and settled back down.

"That's okay," Rachel said. "You go ahead and sleep while I have all the fun. I'll take you for a ride on my skateboard some other time."

Rachel was about to start down the hall again, when a shrill voice called out, "Rachel Yoder, what are you doing?"

Rachel whirled around so fast, she lost control

of the skateboard. It sailed across the floor, and Rachel fell hard, landing on both knees. "Ouch! Ouch!"

Mom rushed up the stairs to Rachel. "Are you hurt?"

"Jah, my knees are bleeding."

"And see here what you've done." Mom pointed to a hole near the hem of Rachel's dress.

Rachel wiggled on the floor, trying not to cry. "I—I didn't do it on purpose."

"Calm down," Mom said softly as she examined Rachel's knees. "I can't help if you don't stay still."

"If I'd been wearing pants like English girls get to wear, I probably wouldn't have gotten hurt," Rachel complained.

"There will be no more of that kind of talk," Mom said crossly. "Now stop with the *rutschich* and let me take a closer look at the damage you've done."

"I can't help it if I'm squirming." Rachel sniffed. "My knees hurt awfully."

"You brought this trouble on yourself. You know better than to ride your skateboard in the house." Mom pointed to the hardwood floor. "Now look at what you've done to my freshly polished floor."

Rachel hadn't noticed all the ugly streaks her

skateboard had left. She felt sad because she knew she had marred Mom's clean floor. "I'm sorry," she cried as tears seeped under her lashes and splashed onto her cheeks. Her knees hurt, and she felt so ashamed that she didn't even care if Jacob heard about this and called her a crybaby.

"Sorry is good, but you must learn a lesson," Mom said, shaking her head. "You need to start thinking about what you're doing and stay out of trouble. As soon as we clean and bandage your knees, you will have to scrub and repolish the floor. And then you may try out your new sewing kit on the hole you put in your dress."

The last thing Rachel wanted to do was mend her dress, but she knew better than to argue with Mom—especially after she had messed up the shiny, clean floor. She glanced at Cuddles, who was still asleep in the corner of the hall. It was a good thing the kitten hadn't been on the skateboard with her when she fell. It was bad enough that she had injured her knees. She wouldn't have wanted Cuddles to get hurt, too.

Mom helped Rachel to her feet. "No more skateboarding in the house. Do you understand?"

Rachel nodded and stared at the floor. "Where can I skate?"

"I don't know where would be a good place, but

I think trying to balance on a silly old skateboard is just asking for trouble."

"A lot of kinner have them. I've seen many of the English kinner ride skateboards in town."

Mom frowned. "You know, Rachel, some folks believe other people's bread tastes better than their own."

Rachel knew that Mom meant it wasn't good to always want the things others had. But was it really so wrong for her to want a skateboard?

Mom pointed to Cuddles. "You know the cat's not supposed to be in the house."

"Sorry," Rachel mumbled.

After Mom cleaned up Rachel's knees and bandaged them, Rachel spent the next hour cleaning and polishing the hallway floor. By the time she had finished, she wondered if having a skateboard was worth so much trouble.

Esther and Rudy showed up while Rachel sat at the kitchen table, mending her dress. "Sorry I wasn't here to wish you a happy birthday this morning," Esther said before she leaned over Rachel's chair and kissed the top of her head.

Rudy placed a large paper sack on the table. "It's my fault your sister was gone so long. We hired a driver to take us to Lancaster so we could do some shopping."

Rachel shrugged. It really didn't matter that her big sister hadn't been there when she opened her presents this morning. She didn't even care that Esther hadn't given her anything. Rachel's day was ruined the moment she'd fallen off the skateboard and discovered that she'd marred Mom's floor.

Esther looked around the room. "Where's the rest of the family?"

"Mom's upstairs, checking the hallway floor I just polished. Pap, Henry, and Jacob are working in the fields." Rachel set her sewing aside and stood.

"Why did you polish the hallway floor?" her sister asked. "I thought Mom did that yesterday."

Rachel nodded. "She did, but I scuffed it with my new skateboard."

"Skateboard?" Rudy's dark eyebrows drew together, and he glanced at Esther with a strange look on his face.

"Jah," Rachel explained. "I couldn't find any place to skate on it, so I tried the hallway upstairs."

Esther pointed to the paper sack Rudy had placed on the table. "You may as well open this, Rachel, because you'll probably want to take it back right away."

Rachel peered inside the sack and gasped. "Another skateboard?"

Esther nodded. "I knew you'd wanted one for a long time."

"We stopped at a toy store in Lancaster this morning and bought it," Rudy added.

Rachel just stood there, too stunned to utter a word. Finally, she began to laugh. She laughed and laughed until tears rolled down her cheeks and her sides ached.

"Do you think this is funny?" Esther tipped her head and gave Rachel a curious look.

Rachel hiccupped on another chuckle. "It *is* funny. I woke up this morning owning one half a skateboard, and now I own two more!"

Rudy's eyebrows lifted high on his forehead. "Huh?"

"I didn't think anyone would buy me a skateboard for my birthday," Rachel explained. "So a few weeks ago I put one on layaway at Kauffman's."

"You did?" Esther touched Rachel's shoulder.

"Jah, but I didn't have enough money to get the skateboard off layaway. Then this morning, Jacob and Henry gave me a wooden skateboard they had made for my birthday. Now, you and Rudy have just given me—"

"Another skateboard," Esther said, finishing Rachel's sentence. "Oh, little sister, that *is* funny!"

"I haven't told anyone else in the family about the skateboard I planned to buy myself," Rachel said in a whisper. "I didn't want to hurt Jacob's and Henry's feelings, because they must have worked hard on the one they made." She leaned over and touched her sore knees. "And now the skateboard they gave me has caused so much trouble, I almost wish I didn't have any!"

"Today was a day for learning lessons, wasn't it, sister?" asked Esther.

"Jah," Rachel replied with a nod.

"Say, I have an idea. Why don't you return the skateboard we gave you and use the money you get back to buy something else?" Rudy suggested.

"That probably would be best. And I'll cancel my layaway on the other skateboard." Rachel drew in a quick breath and released it with a huff. "Now if I can just find a good place to ride the one skateboard I'm going to keep."

"How about the barn?" Rudy asked. "There should be plenty of room in there for you to skateboard."

Rachel shook her head. "I already thought of that, but too many bales of hay are stacked in the barn."

Rudy smiled. "I don't think that's a problem. I'll go to the fields and see your daed. If he says it's okay, I'll move some of the bales out of the way so you'll have enough room to skateboard."

"That's a wunderbaar idea," Esther said excitedly. "And I'll help Rudy move them."

Rachel gave Esther and Rudy both a hug. She had gotten a new skateboard, would soon have a place to ride it, and tonight they would probably have a barbecue supper. This had turned out to be a pretty good birthday after all.

Chapter 9

Dunner and Wedderleech

Rachel looked forward to sharing a meal with her family at Uncle Ben and Aunt Irma's home. Uncle Ben was Pap's older brother. Mary was Uncle Ben and Aunt Irma's youngest daughter—and Rachel's favorite cousin. She hoped that after supper she and Mary would have time to play on the swing hanging from the rafters in the barn.

"Sure wish I could have brought Cuddles along," Rachel said from her seat in the back of the buggy. "She would have enjoyed playing with Mary's cat, Stripes."

"Maybe some other time, Rachel," Mom called over her shoulder. "After your kitten gets used to riding in the buggy."

"That was disgusting when you brought that critter along on a ride last time, and she threw up."

Jacob wrinkled his nose. "Just thinking about *kotze* is enough to make my stomach flip-flop. Your cat is as much trouble as you are!"

"Let's have no more of that talk," Pap scolded. "We don't need to ruin our appetites."

"That's right," Henry agreed. "Cousin Abe told me his daed's fixing homemade ice cream for dessert, and I hope to eat at least two bowls."

"Me, too," Jacob agreed. "I might even have three bowls."

"What a pig," Rachel mumbled. "Oink, oink."

Jacob poked her on the arm. "Look who's talking. The last time Mom made ginger cookies, you ate half a dozen before I finished one."

"Did not."

"Did so."

"Did not."

Esther turned in her seat and put her finger to her lips.

Rachel knew her sister wasn't trying to be bossy. She probably didn't want Rachel or Jacob to get in trouble this evening.

Not that Jacob would get in trouble, Rachel thought. *I'm the only one who gets in trouble around here!*

So for the rest of the ride, Rachel remained quiet, watching the scenery and dreaming about riding in a fast car with the top down.

Soon they were pulling into Uncle Ben's place, and before long, everyone had found seats at the picnic tables in the backyard. Rachel sat beside Mary and her older sister, Nancy. Jacob sat between his cousins Abe and Sam. Henry and Esther sat at the table with the grown-ups.

Besides barbecued hot dogs and burgers, the families could choose from coleslaw, cucumber slices, cherry tomatoes, macaroni salad, potato chips, and ice-cold lemonade.

"God is good. Let us thank Him for what He gives to us," Uncle Ben said before all bowed their heads for silent prayer.

The meal was tasty, and everyone seemed happy. After the meal, Rachel and Mary were about to walk to the barn, when a cloud burst open and rain began to fall.

"Looks like we might be in for another summer storm," Pap said.

"We'd better clear this table quickly." Mom grabbed empty dishes, and everyone else did the same.

"Even though it's raining, we can still go to the barn," Mary said as she and Rachel raced for the house with their hands full of empty bowls. When everything had been cleared away, the girls headed for the barn.

Boom! Crack! Thunder clapped, and lightning zigzagged across the sky. Rachel shuddered. She only feared a few things, and lightning was one of them.

"Come on, let's run!" Mary grabbed Rachel's hand and pulled her across the yard.

"I hope the rain stops soon," Rachel panted as the girls entered the barn. "We had enough rain when summer first began."

"Think how nice and fresh the air smells after it rains." Mary scampered up to the hayloft, and Rachel followed. If the storm got any worse, she didn't want to be alone.

"Sure wish I didn't have to wear this dress," she complained. "It would be a lot easier to climb if I could wear trousers like Jacob."

Mary grunted. "You wouldn't really want to dress like a boy, would you?"

Rachel shrugged. "Have you ever wondered how God dresses?"

Her cousin smiled. "Maybe He wears all the love everyone gives Him."

"You might be right." Rachel looked around the hayloft. "Say, where's your cat? I thought Stripes liked to sleep up here."

Mary flopped onto a pile of straw. "He does, but if he isn't tired, he could be most anywhere."

"He wouldn't be outside when it's raining, would he?"

"Probably not. He might be here somewhere, trying to catch a mouse." Mary tugged Rachel's hand. "Have a seat, and we can talk while we listen to the rain hit the roof."

Thunder boomed again, and Rachel trembled. "Maybe we should go back to the house."

"Aw, come on. Don't be so naerfich. We'll be fine."

"I'm not nervous. I'm just a little bit afraid." With a gusty sigh, Rachel sank to her knees beside her cousin.

"What is it about the rain that makes you so scared?" Mary asked.

"It's not the rain, it's the dunner and wedderleech I don't like," Rachel replied.

Mary lifted her hands toward the ceiling. "God made the thunder and lightning, so why be afraid?"

"I know the dunner won't hurt me. It just sounds bad when it echoes through the sky." Rachel plucked up a piece of straw and twirled it around her fingers as she fought the urge to bite off a nail. "It's the wedderleech that worries me."

"How come?"

Rachel frowned. "Pap told us the other day that he heard about a man who had been struck by lightning."

Mary's eyes grew wide. "Did he—"

"No, the man didn't die, but he had burns on his body, and all of his hair turned white." Rachel touched the side of her head. "I don't know what I would do if my blond hair suddenly turned white."

"Rachel! Mary! Where are you?" The voice interrupted the conversation.

"We're up here, Nancy," Mary called to her sister.

"The ice cream is ready, and Mama sent me to get you."

"Okay, we're coming." Mary and Rachel stood and brushed the hay stubbles from their dresses. They carefully went down the ladder and hurried out of the barn.

In the house, the girls and their families gathered around Aunt Irma's kitchen table, eating creamy homemade ice cream with chocolate topping and fresh strawberries.

Then Pap pushed his chair away from the table and stood. "This has been a most enjoyable evening, but I think it's time for us to go home. The rain isn't letting up, and it's getting dark."

"Do you have to go so soon?" Mary asked with a groan. "I wanted to take Rachel to my room and show her the doll I'm making."

"You can show her some other time," Mary's father said.

Everyone said good-bye, and as Pap hitched up the horse, the rain pelted the ground even harder.

By the time Rachel's family had pulled onto the highway, lightning filled the night sky. Thunderous roars shook their buggy.

Rachel shivered as she thought about the day she had been trapped in the Millers' root cellar. It had been thundering and lightning then, too.

Esther reached under her seat and grabbed a quilt, which she wrapped around Rachel's shoulders.

"Danki," Rachel said gratefully. She hoped the warmth of the quilt would help her stop shivering.

"Isn't the storm exciting?" Jacob shouted in her ear.

She shook her head. "I don't think so. And don't holler. It makes me more nervous."

"Aw, you're just an old scaredy-cat. You've always been that way, but it's been worse since you got locked in the Millers' cellar."

Rachel didn't understand why her brother chose a time like this to tease. Bad storms were no laughing matter. She looked at him and squinted her eyes. "Maybe someone should lock you in a cellar, and then we'll see how brave you are!"

Mom turned in her seat at the front of the buggy and looked sternly at both of them over the top of her glasses. "Your daed's having a hard enough time trying to control the horse in this awful weather. He doesn't need you two yelling."

"Sorry," Rachel and Jacob said at the same time.

Pap guided the horse off the main road and onto the graveled driveway leading to their farm, but suddenly, he pulled on the reins. "Whoa, there! Hold steady, boy!"

"What's wrong?" Mom asked.

Pap pointed to the left. "Fire! Our barn is on fire!"

Rachel looked out the rain-streaked window. Sure enough, thick smoke bellowed from their barn, and angry red flames shot high into the sky.

"It must have been struck by the lightning!" Pap hollered. He smacked the reins hard, and for the first time in a long while, old Tom galloped up the driveway. When they reached the yard, Pap stopped the horse and said to Mom, "You'd better drive over to the Johnsons' place, Miriam, and ask them to phone the fire department. Then head to the Millers' and let them know that we could use their help." Pap jumped down from the buggy. Henry, Jacob, and Esther did the same. Rachel just sat there, watching helplessly as her family raced for the buckets sitting near the outside pump.

Mom slid into the driver's seat and reached for the reins. Then she turned to Rachel. "You can either get out and help fill buckets with water or ride with me."

Rachel blinked several times, fighting back tears. "I'll stay and help." She climbed down from the buggy and watched Mom speed out of the yard.

Rachel's legs felt heavy as she stumbled toward the water pump.

The fire burned fast, and Rachel's heart nearly stopped beating when she saw Pap and Henry race into the barn. She breathed a sigh of relief when they returned, leading several animals safely out. Rain and ashes from the fire covered the men's faces. Even Esther, who stood at the pump, filling buckets and handing them to Pap and her brothers, looked a mess.

Rachel noticed that the rain had tapered off. *Why, when we need heavy rain to help stop the fire?* she wondered.

"It's not helping!" Henry gasped as he grabbed another bucket and threw it at the burning flames. "What are we going to do, Pap?"

"Rachel, don't just stand there. Help fill some buckets, schnell!" Pap shouted.

Rachel forced herself to stop shaking and dashed to the pump. The buckets were heavy, and she struggled against the howling wind whipping the hem of her dress. The choking smoke burned Rachel's eyes, and tears stung her hot cheeks.

Pap's barn was important. He kept all the animals there, as well as the alfalfa hay he raised to sell. He couldn't lose it. He just couldn't.

Soon the yard was full of neighbors, both Amish and English. Everyone worked hard, dumping buckets of cold water onto the angry, burning flames.

The wind grew stronger, and the fire spread quickly throughout the barn. The fire trucks still hadn't arrived.

Rachel gasped when old Tom trotted into the yard with no buggy and no Mom. Should she tell Pap or let him keep working? She didn't want to worry him, but if something had happened to Mom— Even though Rachel felt she caused a lot of trouble for her mother and that Mom often punished her, Rachel loved her mother very much.

Finally, Pap signaled the men to stop, and Rachel stood with the others and watched Pap's barn burn to the ground. The fire trucks arrived at last, but it was too late.

Rachel stepped up to her father, ready to tell him that old Tom had returned without Mom, when another buggy pulled into the yard. Anna Miller got out, and so did Rachel's mother.

"Mom! Where have you been?" Rachel shouted. "What happened to our buggy?"

"Old Tom broke away when we tried to put him in the Millers' barn," Mom explained. "He seemed so jittery on the drive over that I decided to leave him there and ride back in Anna's buggy."

"I'm glad you're all right," Rachel said, hugging her mother.

Mom nodded and patted Rachel's head. "I'm fine, but I see our barn didn't do so well." She reached for Pap's hand as he stepped beside her. "Did you get all the animals out, Levi?"

"Jah," he mumbled. "I believe so."

"It will be okay," Mom whispered. "We'll ask our friends and neighbors to help us rebuild."

"I've helped others rebuild." Pap slowly shook his head. "But in all the years we've been married, this is the first barn I have ever lost."

"When trouble comes, we must not be too proud to ask for help," Mom said with a catch in her voice.

Pap nodded. "You're right, Miriam. I will ask."

Rachel wished she could do or say something to make Pap feel better. At least he'd been able to get the animals out. That was a good thing.

Then sudden panic struck Rachel. *Cuddles! Where is Cuddles?* Had her sweet little bussli been in the barn when it caught fire?

Rachel cupped her hands around her mouth and hollered, "Has anyone seen my kitten?"

Chapter 10

Barn Raising

Pap, Henry, Jacob, and several Amish men who lived nearby spent the next few days cleaning up the mess from the burned-out barn.

On Friday, when Rachel came downstairs to help with breakfast, first she opened the back door and called for Cuddles. Rachel called for Cuddles many times every day, but the kitten was still missing. Rachel only saw a yard full of Amish men and boys who'd come to help raise the new barn. Mom had said probably a hundred or more would help, and Rachel was sure at least that many had arrived already.

"I guess Pap will have plenty of help today," she said to Esther, who had just finished setting the table.

Her sister nodded. "Even many of our English

neighbors have come to help. All the men will be busy today preparing the planks, panels, rafters, and beams that will make up Pap's new barn."

"Since the table's already set, what would you like me to do?" Rachel asked, stepping to the counter where her mother stood cracking eggs into a bowl.

"I could use a few more eggs, so why don't you run out to the chicken coop and see how many you can find?"

Rachel frowned. "Oh, Mom, do I have to? You know the trouble I have when I try to gather eggs."

"Just watch what you're doing, and I'm sure you'll be fine." Mom nudged Rachel toward the door.

With a weary sigh, Rachel trudged across the yard toward the chicken coop. She was relieved when everything went okay and she found six plump eggs. None of the hens gave her a bit of trouble, either.

She headed back across the lawn but almost tripped on some boards that were to be used on the barn. She grunted and moved on until Frank Johnson, one of their English neighbors, asked if she would bring him a drink of water.

Rachel set the basket of eggs on one of the wooden tables and hurried to the pump. She grabbed a paper cup from the stack sitting there, filled it with water, and took it to Mr. Johnson.

He smiled and took a drink. "That hit the spot. Thanks."

"You're welcome." Rachel rushed back to the table where she had left the basket, only to discover that it was gone. "Have you seen my basket of eggs?" she asked Jacob when he walked by carrying a hammer and a can of nails.

He shook his head and kept walking.

Rachel questioned several other people, but no one had seen the eggs.

"Always trouble somewhere," she muttered as she headed to the house.

"How'd it go in the chicken coop?" Mom asked when Rachel entered the kitchen empty-handed. "Didn't you get any eggs?"

"I collected six." Rachel grunted. "But I set the basket on one of the tables so I could get Frank Johnson a cup of water, and when I got back, the basket was gone."

Mom's pale eyebrows lifted, and she peered at Rachel over the top of her glasses. "Where did it go?"

"I have no idea." Rachel moved toward her mother. "I told you I didn't want to collect the eggs."

"There has to be some explanation. Did you ask

the men if they had seen the basket?"

Rachel nodded. "Nobody knew anything about it. Now the eggs are missing, and so is my cat."

"I'm sure Cuddles is just hiding someplace," Mom said with a shake of her head. "But someone must know what happened to the basket of eggs. Baskets don't jump off the table and walk away by themselves."

"I–I'll go back outside and look again." Rachel was beginning to believe that *she* was the trouble. Maybe she had set the basket somewhere else and didn't remember doing it. She had been kind of forgetful this summer.

"That's okay. I'll make do with the eggs I already have," her mother said. "Our menfolk ate earlier, so everyone's had breakfast except you, me, and Esther."

Rachel glanced around the kitchen. "Where is Esther? She was here when I went to the chicken coop. I hope my *schweschder* isn't missing now, too."

"Your sister isn't missing. She just went outside to say hello to Rudy."

"That's good." Rachel moved to the sink to wash her hands. "At least I know I'm not to blame for Cuddles being missing."

Mom made no comment. She just placed a frying pan on the stove and started cooking the eggs she already had.

A few minutes later, the back door opened, and Esther stepped into the kitchen, carrying a wicker basket.

"Where'd you find that?" Rachel asked.

"Outside on one of the tables."

"Which one?"

"The table closest to where the new barn's going to be." Esther set the basket near Mom.

"I didn't put it on that table. I'm sure I set the basket on the table nearest the pump. Someone must have moved it." Rachel squinted. "I wonder if Jacob—"

"It's not important," Mom said, waving her hand. "We have our eggs now, and that's all that matters."

Rachel grunted. If Jacob had taken the eggs, he should be punished. But Mom probably didn't even care. Rachel felt that she always got scolded for the things she did, and Jacob got away with everything.

By noon, the skeleton of the barn had begun to take shape, rising high above the ground. The Pennsylvania Dutch language drifted up from the work site as men and boys pounded nails, cut boards, and fit them securely in place.

Rachel joined Mom, Esther, and several other women in the kitchen while they prepared lunch for the workers. The tables were filled with meatloaf sandwiches, several kinds of salad, pickles, olives, potato chips, and plenty of iced tea, water, and lemonade. For dessert, they could enjoy gingerbread and a variety of cookies. Since the weather was still warm, everyone ate outside at the tables. During the meal, the men even took time to visit and tell jokes. Even when disaster struck, whether it was big or little, Rachel was learning, you kept going and made the best of things.

"Say, where's your straw hat?" Jacob asked Pap as he selected another slice of gingerbread.

Pap grabbed a couple of peanut butter cookies and said, "I took it off when I washed up at the pump. It must be over there still."

"Not anymore." Jacob pointed to one of the beams overhead. "Look there, Pap. Someone nailed your hat to the new barn!"

Pap tipped his head and squinted against the glare of the sun. A huge smile crept across his bearded face. "All right now—who's the *galgedieb*?"

A few Amish boys sitting nearby snickered, but nobody said who the scoundrel was. For once Rachel was glad she hadn't done anything wrong.

"That's all right. My head was getting too warm

anyway." Pap glanced at Rachel and winked. Then he chuckled.

Rachel gritted her teeth as she helped clear away the dishes. Maybe Jacob hadn't moved her basket of eggs. It was probably those same teasing boys who had nailed Pap's hat to the barn. She was tempted to scold them, but Mom called her to join the women and girls at the picnic tables.

When the meal was over, Rachel and Mary hurried to the creek. They sat under a willow tree, and Rachel leaned against the tree trunk.

"Sure is nice to see how many folks have come to help build your daed's new barn," Mary said.

Rachel nodded. "I know Pap appreciates it, but it doesn't seem fair that we lost the barn."

"I heard my daed say the other day that trouble can make us stronger and teaches us to call on God."

Rachel groaned. "I've been calling on Him ever since the fire, but I don't think He's listening."

"What's wrong?" Mary asked.

"I'm worried about my kitten."

Mary frowned. "Where is Cuddles? I haven't seen her today."

"The last time I saw her was the morning before the barn burned down." Rachel bit her bottom lip to keep it from trembling. Thinking about her kitten made her feel so sad. "What if Cuddles was trapped inside the barn when it caught fire?"

Mary gasped. "That would be *baremlich*."

Rachel nodded. "It would be worse than terrible."

"Should we go look for her?"

"I've looked and called for her every day, but there's no sign of Cuddles anywhere." Rachel's eyes burned with tears, and she blinked to keep them from spilling over. "I don't believe she's ever coming back. I think I've lost her for good."

Mary held Rachel's hand and gently squeezed it. "Don't say that. I'll help you search for the bussli. Maybe she's someplace you haven't already looked."

"Jah, maybe so."

Rachel and Mary spent the rest of the afternoon looking for Cuddles, but they couldn't find her. They finally decided to give up and go to the house for cookies and milk.

Shortly before suppertime, the workers went home. Many promised to return the next day to help Pap put the final touches on his new barn.

Rachel asked her mother if Mary could spend the night.

Mom looked over at her sister-in-law. "What do you think about that idea?"

Aunt Irma nodded. "Jah, sure. It's fine with me."

Rachel hugged her cousin, and the two of them jumped up and down. Rachel thought having her cousin spend the night might help her forget about her missing kitten. At least it would keep her too busy to think about it so much.

"Calm down, Mary," Aunt Irma said with a click of her tongue. "You be sure and help Rachel with her chores."

Mary nodded. "I will, Mama."

The girls stood on the porch, watching as the last buggy pulled out of the Yoders' yard. Then they ran into the house, giggling.

That evening after they'd eaten supper and all the dishes had been washed, dried, and put away, Mom turned to the girls and said, "You'd best take a bath before you head upstairs to bed."

"Oh, Mom," Rachel groaned. "We're not that dirty."

"I just washed your bedsheets, and I don't want any filthy little bodies soiling them tonight."

Rachel knew she wouldn't win this argument, so she trudged down the hallway toward the bathroom, with Mary right behind her.

When the girls awoke the following morning, the men were already hard at work. The piercing sound of hammers and saws echoed through Rachel's open window.

Mary yawned and pulled the sheet over her head. "It can't be time to get up already."

Rachel opened one eye and squinted at the sun streaming in through the crack of the dark window shade. "I'm afraid the sun is almost over the barn already. I guess we should have gone to bed a little earlier last night."

"We'd better hurry and get dressed," Mary said as she swung her legs over the side of the bed. "Your mamm and Esther will need our help."

The girls entered the kitchen just as a knock sounded on the back door. Mom opened it, and Jake Miller entered, carrying Rachel's kitten in his arms.

"Cuddles!" Rachel cried. She raced to Jake, and he handed her the squirming animal. "Where have you been, you silly bussli?"

"I found her over at our place this morning, playing in the flower beds with Missy and her other busslin," Jake said.

"Do you think she got scared when the storm blew in and headed back to the place where she was born?" Rachel's mother asked.

Jake nodded. "That's what my daed believes happened. The cat's probably been there the whole time, and we didn't see her until today."

Tears welled in Rachel's eyes as relief washed over her like a spring rain. "Danki for bringing Cuddles back to me, Jake."

"You're welcome."

She kissed the tip of the kitten's nose. "At least you knew what to do when trouble came. Welcome home, my furry little friend."

Chapter 11

Out to Pasture

Rachel's eyes felt heavy, and she leaned her head against the seat in the back of their buggy. They had been to the public auction so Pap could buy some things he needed for the new barn. Now it seemed to be taking them forever to get home.

"Why are we stopping again?" Jacob complained.

Rachel opened one eye and looked at him. "Ask Pap. He's the driver."

"It must be our stupid horse," her brother said, wrinkling his nose. "Every couple of miles old Tom stops in the road. When he does decide to go, he plods along like a turtle. That horse isn't worth much anymore. I think we should get rid of him."

Rachel sat up straight. "No way! Tom may be a little slow, but he's a good horse. It wouldn't be right for Pap to sell him."

Jacob nudged her arm. "The old horse will probably end up at the glue factory. Jah, that's where Pap should take him, all right."

Rachel's mouth dropped open. "How can you say that? Turning our trusty horse into a pile of glue would be terrible!"

"Oh, don't let Jacob rile you," said Henry, who sat in the seat ahead of them, reading a book. "More than likely Pap will just put old Tom out to pasture."

Rachel tapped Henry on the shoulder. "Out to pasture? What does that mean?"

"It means that since the horse isn't good for anything, he'll be put in the empty fields to spend the rest of his days alone," Jacob said before Henry could answer.

"But that's not true," Rachel argued. "Tom is good for lots of things."

Jacob snorted. "Name one."

Rachel rested her chin in the palm of her hand. "Let me see. . . ."

"You can't think of anything, can you?"

"Give me a minute, and I'll come up with something." Rachel squeezed her eyes shut and thought hard. A few minutes later, her eyes snapped open. "I've got one."

"What is it?"

"Tom is good for petting because he's nice and tame and doesn't bite."

"Being good to pet doesn't make him useful to Pap."

"Well, he's useful to me." Rachel pouted. "I love old Tom, and if he's put out to pasture, then I'm going with him!"

Jacob shook his head and muttered something about Rachel being *lecherlich*.

I'm not ridiculous, Rachel thought. *You're just mean!*

She closed her eyes again and tried to relax, but she could only think about their poor buggy horse and what might happen to him. By the time they got home, she decided to talk with Pap.

Rachel waited until everyone else had left the buggy and headed for the house. Then she hopped down and sprinted around to where Pap was unhitching the horse.

"Can I speak to you a minute?" she asked, stepping beside him.

"Jah, sure. What's on your mind?"

"It's about old Tom."

Pap's eyes narrowed. "That horse has been nothing but trouble for me these days. He's through pulling our buggy."

"Oh, but, Pap—"

"I mean it, Rachel. Old Tom gets tired and either walks too slow or stops in the middle of the road whenever he wants. I'm afraid he's finished."

Tears filled Rachel's eyes, blurring her vision. "You—you mean you're going to sell him to the glue factory?"

Pap tipped his head and looked at Rachel as if she had lost her mind. "Where did you ever get that idea?"

She sniffed and reached out to pat the horse's neck. "Jacob said you might sell him to the glue factory."

"You should know I'd never do that." Pap stroked the end of Tom's nose, and the horse nuzzled his hand. "I'm going to put this old fellow out to pasture."

"No, Pap, please don't do that," Rachel pleaded. "Tom wouldn't like being out there all alone."

"He won't be alone," Pap said as he led the horse toward the barn. "My workhorses will be in the pasture with Tom when they're not helping me and the boys in the fields. And Sam, my other buggy horse, will join them sometimes, too."

Rachel followed Pap and Tom into the barn. "So putting the horse out to pasture isn't a bad thing?"

Pap shook his head. "It just means he'll take life a little easier from now on."

"You mean like Grandma and Grandpa Yoder who live in the *daadihaus* next door to Uncle Ben and Aunt Irma's?"

"That's right. Grandma and Grandpa can't do all the things they used to, and they're not expected to work as hard anymore." Pap smiled. "Since they live in the grandfather's house next to your uncle Ben, they're never lonely, and someone is always close by to care for their needs."

Rachel sat on a bale of hay while Pap removed the dirt and sweat from old Tom with a currycomb and brush. "How soon do you plan to put the horse out to pasture?" she asked.

Pap gave the horse's flanks a gentle pat. "Probably tomorrow morning."

"And he'll stay there and never be allowed in the barn again?"

Pap shook his head. "He'll be out in the pasture during the day and spend his nights in here, same as always."

"Hmm. . ." Rachel decided she would think of some way to make Tom's retirement days more pleasant. She thought about Grandma and Grandpa, too, and how she wanted to do something special to let them know how much she loved them.

The following day, Rachel asked Mom if she could have an apple and some carrots to take out to the pasture and give to old Tom. Mom said it was okay, so a few minutes later Rachel hurried out the back door, carrying a plastic bag with some carrots and an apple inside. When she reached the pasture, she found Tom lying under a tree near the fence. The old horse got up and wandered over to greet her as soon as she called his name.

"Are you lonely, boy?" Rachel asked, climbing the fence and seating herself on the top rail so she could pet the horse.

Tom neighed in response and nudged Rachel's hand.

"I brought you a treat," she said, holding a carrot out to him.

Tom chomped it hungrily and nudged her hand again.

"Okay, okay. Don't be in such a hurry," she said with a chuckle.

After Tom had finished the second carrot, she reached into the bag and offered him the apple. "Now this is your dessert."

Tom crunched the apple, snorted, and let out a loud *neigh!* Then he bumped Rachel's hand again with his warm nose.

"I don't have anything else for you," she said.

"If you're still hungry, you'll have to eat some grass. That's why it's here, you know."

Tom twitched his nose and shook his head as if he were telling Rachel he didn't want more grass.

"I've got to go see Grandpa and Grandma Yoder now, but I'll be back tomorrow." She patted the horse's head and was about to climb down when *thud!* The fence shook, pitching Rachel forward.

"Agh!" Off the fence she flew, landing with a *splat* in the horses' watering trough.

Rachel pulled herself up, coughing and spitting water out of her mouth. One of their big billy goats stood on the other side of the fence, shaking its head and baaing so loud that Rachel had to cover her ears.

"Shoo! Shoo! Get on back to the goat pen!" Rachel hollered, waving her hands. "Thanks to you butting the fence, I lost my balance and fell in the water trough."

The goat let out another loud *baa* and ran off.

Rachel crawled out of the trough, wrung the water from her dress, and climbed back over the fence. "Always trouble somewhere," she grumbled as she headed for the house.

Later, dressed in clean, dry clothes, Rachel got Mom's permission to pick a few flowers to take to

Grandma. She had painted a rock for Grandpa and put it inside a canvas bag that she set on the porch while she picked flowers.

After Rachel had a bouquet of pretty pink flowers in one hand, she picked up her canvas bag. She was about to head out, when she spotted Cuddles sitting inside one of Pap's old work boots on the porch. "You silly bussli," she said with a laugh. "What are you doing in there?"

Cuddles looked at Rachel and meowed.

"Are you stuck? Do you need help getting out?" Rachel set the flowers and the canvas bag on the porch step and bent over. She lifted Cuddles by the scruff of her neck, then set the kitten on the porch. "There, now. That's better, isn't it?"

Cuddles jumped back into the boot with another *meow!*

Rachel shook her finger in the kitten's face. "I don't have time to play your silly games. I'm going to see Grandma and Grandpa Yoder now." She plucked Cuddles out of the boot for a second time and set her on the porch.

The kitten leaped into the boot again and stared at Rachel, as if to say, "I dare you to make me move."

Rachel grabbed her canvas bag and the flowers and then stepped off the porch. "You can stay there the rest of the day, for all I care." She headed around the side of the house and stopped to look at a grasshopper sitting on the sidewalk. Suddenly, Cuddles dashed around the corner of the house and pounced on her bare foot. "What's gotten into you today, Cuddles?"

The kitten rolled onto her back and pawed at the air, like she did whenever she wanted Rachel to scratch her stomach.

Rachel stepped around the cat. "Not now, Cuddles. I need to get these flowers over to Grandma before they wilt." She stuck her foot out and nudged the cat a little, but Cuddles leaped up and swiped Rachel's leg with her paw.

Rachel jumped back. "Ouch! Your claws are sharp, and you should be ashamed of yourself for being so mean." Of course, Rachel knew her kitten wasn't really being mean. Cuddles just wanted to play, so she was doing everything possible to get Rachel's attention.

"You seem to find trouble as easily as I do, little bussli. But you don't mean to, and I still love you," Rachel said, patting the kitten's soft fur. "I'm your mother now, and I guess moms always love their babies no matter how much trouble they get into."

Rachel stopped and thought about what she'd just said. She felt terrible whenever she got into trouble with Mom. She was always a little afraid Mom would stop loving her because she caused so many problems. But maybe Mom wasn't any more upset with her than she was with Cuddles.

"I love you no matter what," Rachel told Cuddles. "And I guess Mom loves me, even when I make mistakes."

Cuddles purred and licked the scratch marks she had left on Rachel's leg.

Rachel smiled. "I accept your apology, and if you'd like to go with me to Grandma and Grandpa's house, I'd be happy to have your company."

The kitten meowed and purred louder. Rachel and Cuddles set out on foot, but instead of walking along the road all the way, Rachel decided to take the shortcut through the woods. About halfway there, she spotted some pretty yellow wildflowers blooming near a leafy bush. She picked a few to go with the pink flowers from Mom's garden.

Rachel figured it would be best not to put Cuddles on the ground, because the curious kitten would probably see something that interested her and run off. So she put Cuddles inside her canvas satchel. Then Rachel squatted and picked wildflowers. When she had enough to make a nice bouquet, she removed Cuddles from the satchel and was on her way again.

Soon they were walking up the driveway to Grandma and Grandpa Yoder's house. Because the house was next to Uncle Ben and Aunt Irma's place, Rachel found her cousin Mary in the yard, playing with Stripes.

"What a surprise!" Mary said with a friendly wave. "I didn't know you were coming over today. Did you bring Cuddles so our cats can play together?"

"Actually, I came to see Grandma and Grandpa." Rachel lifted the bouquet she held in one hand. Then she placed Cuddles on the ground. "Maybe the cats can play while I do that."

"Do you want me to watch the cats, or should I go to Grandma and Grandpa's house with you?" Mary asked.

"Maybe it would be best if you stayed with the cats. That way, Cuddles won't be as likely to get into trouble or run off." Rachel scratched a spot on her arm, wondering why it felt so itchy all of a sudden.

"Okay. I'll see you later then." Mary plunked down on the grass between the two cats, and Rachel headed for the daadihaus.

I hope they're not napping, Rachel thought when she knocked on the door and got no response. She set the flowers on the porch swing and was about to leave, when the door opened, and Grandma stuck her head out. "Rachel, what a surprise! Are your folks here with you?"

"No, I walked over by myself. Well, my cat is with me, but she's out in the yard playing with Stripes." Rachel reached for the flowers and handed them to Grandma. "These are for you."

Grandma smiled, and her blue eyes seemed to sparkle more than usual. "How thoughtful of you. Danki, Rachel."

"You're welcome." Rachel reached inside the satchel and removed the painted rock. "This is for Grandpa. I painted it to look like a turtle, because Grandpa likes turtles."

"I'm sure he will be pleased to have this one." Grandma opened the door wider. "Come inside. I made gingerbread this morning. So if you have the time, maybe you can visit while you eat a piece of the bread and drink a glass of cold milk."

"I'd like that." As Rachel entered Grandma's kitchen, a warm, fuzzy feeling came over her. She was glad she had decided to visit her grandparents.

Rachel thought about the Bible verse from 1 John 4:11 that Pap had read to the family a few nights earlier, "Dear friends, since God so loved us, we also ought to love one another."

She liked doing something nice for people. It made her feel happy that she had let Grandma, Grandpa, and even old Tom know how much she loved them. And it made her feel even happier to realize just as she loved Cuddles no matter what, her mother also loved her, even when trouble seemed to find her.

Chapter 12

A New Friend

The afternoon sun beat down on Rachel's head as she trudged wearily across the alfalfa field, carrying a jug of cold tea Mom had asked her to take to the men. To keep her mind off the terrible heat, Rachel let her thoughts wander.

First she thought about the itchy rash on her arm. The morning after she had visited her grandparents, Rachel had discovered the rash and shown it to her mother. "That's poison ivy," Mom had said, clicking her tongue. "How'd you get into that?" Rachel told Mom about picking the wildflowers on the way to Grandma and Grandpa's place. The flowers had been growing near a leafy bush that must have been poison ivy. Mom had put lotion on Rachel's arm and given her a pill to stop the itching, but that had been three days ago, and it still bothered her.

Rachel decided she had better concentrate on something else, because thinking about the rash only made it itch worse.

She thought about the trip she and Pap had made to Lancaster earlier in the week. They'd gone to the toy store so she could return the skateboard Esther and Rudy had given her. Then they'd made a visit to Kauffman's Store, and she'd asked Noah Kauffman to take the green and silver skateboard off layaway and put it back on the shelf so he could sell it to someone else. It had been hard to give up the two shiny skateboards, but she already had one skateboard. Even though the homemade skateboard wasn't nearly as nice as the store-bought ones, she liked it better because her brothers had made it. Rachel had used most of the money she'd gotten back to buy paint and brushes so she could make more pet rocks. She'd also bought a bag of licorice, a drawing tablet, several puzzles, and a flea collar for Cuddles. The kitten was allowed in the house once in a while now, but Mom still didn't want Cuddles to be on Rachel's bed.

Suddenly Cuddles darted between Rachel's legs, causing her to stumble and nearly drop the jug of iced tea. "Cuddles!" she exclaimed. "What are you doing out here?"

The cat looked up at Rachel and let out a pathetic *meow*.

Rachel shook her head. "I can't pick you up. I've got my hands full trying to carry this big jug."

Cuddles trotted beside Rachel through the tall grass. A few minutes later, Rachel spotted Pap, Henry, and Jacob loading mounds of hay onto their wagon. "I brought you something cold to drink," she called.

Pap stopped working and wiped his sweaty forehead with the back of his arm. "You're just in time. I'm thirsty and ready for a little break."

"Me, too," Henry and Jacob agreed.

Rachel handed the jug to Pap. "You'd better go first, because if I give it to Jacob or Henry they might not leave any!" As Pap lifted the jug to his lips, she added, "I forgot to bring paper cups. Sorry about that."

"It's okay," he said with a wink. "I think we can manage." He tilted his head back and poured the cool tea into his mouth. Some of it missed and trickled into his beard, and that made him chuckle. Then Pap handed the jug over to Henry. Then Jacob drank from the jug, too.

"Will you give me and Cuddles a ride back to the house on the wagon?" Rachel asked her father.

"Hop in the back. We're almost ready to take this

load of alfalfa to the barn," he replied. "Then we can get ready to go to market."

Rachel knew Pap was talking about the outdoor market that was being held on the other side of town.

Rachel bent, scooped her kitten into her arms, and climbed into the wagon. She played with Cuddles while the rest of the bales were loaded.

When they were finally ready to go, Jacob climbed in the back with Rachel, while Pap and Henry sat up front. Then Pap started the horses moving through the field toward home.

"Why'd you bring that flea-bitten cat with you?" Jacob asked.

"Cuddles followed me into the field, and I haven't seen any fleh since I bought a flea collar for her."

Jacob pulled a couple pieces of hay from a pile, leaned over, and stuck them behind Rachel's ears. "Now you look like a *butzemann*," he said.

Rachel grabbed the hay and tossed it on the wagon floor. "I'm not a scarecrow, and I'm getting tired of you teasing me, Jacob Yoder."

He winked. "Don't you know that's what brothers are for?"

She folded her arms and frowned. "I'm glad you think so."

"I can't wait to go to the market," Jacob said. He leaned closer to Rachel and whispered, "Say, do you have any birthday money left?"

"Maybe. Why?"

He wiggled his eyebrows. "Thought you could treat me to an ice-cream cone or a root-beer float."

"Why should I when you tease me so?"

"Aw, come on little bensel. You know I'm only funning with you." Jacob grinned. "I'll be nice if you promise to buy me some ice cream."

Rachel rubbed her nose against the kitten's soft fur. "Maybe I will, and maybe I won't!"

When the Yoders arrived at the market a couple of hours later, Rachel was surprised to see the parking lot filled with cars and buggies. People seemed to be walking everywhere.

She climbed out of the buggy as soon as Pap halted the horse. "Is it all right if I walk around and look at some things by myself?" she asked her mother.

"I'd rather you stay with one of us," Mom replied. "It's not good for a young girl to be in a crowd of people by herself."

"She can walk with me," Jacob said with a twinkle in his eye.

Rachel figured her brother only said that because he hoped she would buy him some ice cream. "I'll think about it," she muttered.

"What did you say, Rachel?" Pap asked.

"It was nothing important." She looked up at her father and smiled. "What time should we be back at the buggy?"

"Why don't we meet here at five o'clock?" Mom suggested. "Then we can get a bite to eat on the way home."

"Sounds good to me." Jacob grabbed Rachel's hand and tugged it. "Let's get going, little sister."

As Rachel and Jacob walked away, Rachel spotted an English girl who looked to be about her age. The girl wore blue jeans and a pink T-shirt, and her blond hair was in a ponytail. She held a small, white dog.

"What a cute puppy!" Rachel exclaimed. "What's its name?"

"Bundles. I named him that because he's a bundle of fur. Do you want to pet him?"

Rachel stroked the dog's soft, floppy ears with one hand while Jacob tugged on her other hand and insisted, "Let's go."

Rachel ignored her brother and smiled at the English girl. "I have a kitten named Cuddles, and she's real soft, too."

The girl grinned at Rachel. "My name's Sherry Anderson. What's yours?"

"Rachel Yoder."

"It's nice to meet you, Rachel. Would you like to hold Bundles?"

Rachel nodded, and Jacob elbowed her in the ribs. "I thought we were going for ice cream."

"I never said that. Getting some ice cream was your idea." Rachel took Bundles from Sherry, and she giggled when the pup licked her chin.

"I think he likes you," Sherry said.

"Rachel, are you coming or not?"

Rachel knew Jacob was irritated, because a muscle in his cheek twitched when he squinted his eyes. She reached inside her purse and pulled out two dollars. "I'll stay here and visit with Sherry, and you can go get some ice cream by yourself. How's that sound?"

Jacob hesitated, but then he took the money and hurried off.

"I was about to take Bundles for a walk," Sherry said. "Would you like to come along?"

Rachel made sure Jacob was out of sight. Then she nodded. "I'd like that."

Sherry hooked a leash to her puppy's collar and placed him on the ground. When Bundles tugged on the leash and struggled to run ahead, Rachel figured he might be as eager to go for a walk as she was.

The girls and Bundles moved away from the crowd and headed across the parking lot.

"Sure is a hot day," Sherry commented. "Makes me want to go for a swim."

Rachel smiled. "I like to wade in the creek behind our house when the weather is hot and sticky."

"Another way I cool off is when I go for a ride in my brother's convertible," Sherry said.

Rachel's heart flip-flopped. "Convertible? He has a car with a top he can put down?"

Sherry nodded.

"I've never ridden in a convertible."

"You haven't?"

"No, just our neighbor's van whenever Pap hires him to take us somewhere we can't go in our buggy." Rachel swatted at a fly that seemed determined to land on her nose and tried not to scratch the patch of poison ivy on her arm. "I've always wondered what it would be like to ride in a car with the top down. Does your brother's car go real fast?"

Sherry nodded. "Sometimes. . .when we're on the highway."

Rachel was about to comment, when an English woman tapped her on the shoulder. "Would you mind posing for a picture, little girl?" She lifted her camera and pointed it at Rachel, but Rachel turned her head.

"I only want to snap a couple of shots," the woman insisted.

"I'm sorry, but no," Rachel mumbled.

"Are you sure? I'll pay you a dollar."

Rachel stared at the ground as she thought. *It would be nice to earn a dollar. And I wouldn't have to do anything except pose for a picture to get it.*

She looked at the woman and started to shake her head, when her new friend spoke up. "You can take my picture." Sherry flipped her ponytail, tipped her head, and presented a cheesy smile.

"Humph!" The woman turned and walked away.

"I think that lady must have a fly up her nose," Sherry said.

Rachel giggled. "Thanks for sticking up for me."

"Sure, no problem. I know that the Amish don't like to have their pictures taken."

Rachel wondered what Jacob would have done if he had been there. *Probably would have teased me and said, "Who'd want to take* your *picture, little butzemann?"*

Rachel's thoughts were interrupted when a deep voice called from across the parking lot, "Hey, Sherry. Mom just called on my cell phone, and she wants us to come home."

Sherry looked over at Rachel and stuck out her lower lip. "That's my brother, Dave. I guess it's time for me to go."

"Maybe we'll meet again sometime."

Sherry nodded. "I hope so."

As Rachel started across the parking lot toward their buggy, she smiled, thinking about how nice it was to have met someone new. Maybe sometime in the future, she and Sherry would see each other again. And maybe one day, Rachel might get the chance to ride in a shiny blue convertible.

When Rachel reached their buggy, she realized that none of her family had arrived yet, so she climbed into the back, stretched out on the seat, and closed her eyes. It was time to daydream.

Rachel imagined herself riding in a blue convertible with her new friend, Sherry. Sherry's brother drove the car. Bundles and Cuddles sat in the backseat between Rachel and Sherry. The wind whipped the narrow ties of Rachel's kapp as the car whizzed down the highway.

Rachel felt her body sway, first to one side, then to the other, and her eyes snapped open. She sat up and looked out the window. She wasn't riding in a convertible at all. The buggy was moving! She glanced up front to see who was driving but saw no one in the driver's seat.

Rachel realized that Sam, the horse that had taken old Tom's place, must have broken loose from the hitching rail. Now he was galloping across the parking lot. The buggy passed a group of cars, bouncing up and down, weaving this way and that. Rachel screamed when it nearly scraped the side of a green van.

"Whoa, there! Whoa, Sam!" she shouted, but the horse kept running.

I need to get to the front of the buggy and grab those reins! Rachel thought.

She tried to stand up, but the buggy jerked again, and she fell to the floor.

Rachel crawled to the front seat on her hands and knees. She grabbed the back of the seat and started to climb over it. Suddenly, the horse darted to the left, tossing Rachel to the floor again.

"Help!" she screamed as tears rolled down her cheeks. She knew she couldn't do this alone. She really was in trouble now!

"I'm coming, Rachel! Hang on!"

With the racket of the runaway buggy, Rachel barely heard Jacob's voice. She pulled herself up again and looked out the side window. She saw Jacob running beside the buggy. He waved one hand and held an ice-cream cone in the other.

"Help me, Jacob!" Rachel cried.

Jacob tossed the ice-cream cone to the ground and raced past Rachel's window. "Whoa, there! Steady, boy!" he called to the horse.

Rachel's heartbeat pounded with the rhythm of

the horse's hooves. "Dear God," she prayed as she clung to the seat, "please help my brother catch the horse!"

Suddenly the buggy lurched to a screeching halt. Jacob stuck his head through the doorway on the driver's side. He waited a moment, panting.

"I grabbed the horse's bridle and stopped him," he explained, still trying to catch his breath. "I'll lead him back to the hitching rail, so sit tight until I say it's safe to get out."

"Okay," Rachel said in a quavering voice.

When the buggy finally quit moving, Jacob came around to the back and helped Rachel down. "Are you all right?"

Rachel nodded. She could tell her brother was concerned, because his forehead was wrinkled and his eyebrows were drawn together. Ever since school had let out for the summer, Jacob had been teasing her. But now she knew how much her brother really cared. He'd proven that by coming to her rescue, and she was glad for his help.

"I didn't do anything silly, Jacob," she cried. The words tumbled out of her mouth so fast she didn't even know what she was saying. "I was waiting for everyone in the buggy and fell asleep. I don't know how Sam got loose, but I woke up and he was running. I couldn't stop him."

Rachel threw her arms around Jacob. "Danki. Danki for saving my life."

"You're welcome," he said, patting Rachel on the back. "I knew you didn't cause Sam to run away. I tease you about being silly, but I know you are pretty smart for a girl your age."

Jacob seemed embarrassed and ready to change the subject. He looked at his empty hands. "I had my root-beer float and was bringing you an ice-cream cone, but I threw it away so I could stop the horse."

She grinned at him, feeling happier than she had all summer. "That's okay. Knowing that you care about me is better than any old ice-cream cone."

"Of course I care. I'm your brother. I'll always love you and try to help whenever you're in trouble."

"I love you, too." Rachel hugged Jacob again.

"Maybe after supper, Pap will buy us all ice cream," he said with a lopsided grin.

She nodded and smiled. In spite of all her troubles, this summer had turned out to be pretty good, and the best thing was learning that Jacob didn't think she was a bensel. Not really. He did love her after all.